ONLY BY GRACE

ELIZABETH JOHNS

Copyright © 2024 by Elizabeth Johns
Cover Design by 17 Studio Book Design
Edited by Scott Moreland
Historical Content by Heather King

ISBN: 978-1960794253

All rights reserved.
No part of this book may be reproduced in any form or by any electronic or mechanical means, including information storage and retrieval systems, without written permission from the author, except for the use of brief quotations in a book review.

CHAPTER 1

*W*ere it not for the dreadful pounding in her head, Grace would have enjoyed the wedding. For her, it had come as quite a surprise that Patience and Major Stuart had fallen in love. They had always seemed to be bickering more like siblings. But love was a funny notion, and now they wished to be married in a most unusual way due to their experiences that brought them together. It was most romantic, actually, being wed on a ship. At least, it seemed like it would be romantic if it were her own wedding and her head did not feel as though someone was stabbing it with a thousand knives... and if she hadn't taken the draught that her maid had given her which now made her drowsy.

"You do not look very well. Are you seasick?" her sister, Joy, remarked with her usual candour while simultaneously petting one of the kittens that her cat Freddy had recently borne. There were others hidden within the pouch that she wore for that purpose.

"I do not feel very well, thank you very much. The Battle of Trafalgar is happening inside my head at the moment."

"A megrim? The ceremony is over. No one will notice if you go have a lie down," Faith, the eldest sister, suggested as she overheard what Grace and Joy were saying.

The thought of finding a dark corner of the ship and closing her eyes was so appealing that Grace gave no other consideration as to what it might entail.

"You know nothing else works but to sleep it off. Here, take Theodore for company. He is very sweet." Joy handed the black ball of fur to Grace, and he began purring immediately as she held him to her chest.

"You are certain this one is a boy?" She somehow had the presence of mind to ask, not that it mattered.

"I know what to look for now." In their naïveté, they had thought for some time that the mother cat, Freddy, was a boy. Until she gave birth to kittens, that was. Joy then took her hand and asked one of the crew where Grace could go to rest. Grace followed blindly, because it hurt too much to think.

He led them across the deck and down a narrow ladder to a wood-panelled corridor with a few closed doors.

The central one at the end was labelled *Captain*. He opened the door to the right of that, which revealed a small, but tidy, room with a bed, a desk, and a cupboard.

"No one will bother you in here, miss. It's the first mate's cabin and he is not with us this trip."

Grace needed no further encouragement as Joy helped her climb into the berth. After discarding her bonnet, she lay back and closed her eyes as Joy removed her slippers and pulled a coverlet over her. A purring kitten was tucked next to her chest as the darkness and the gentle swaying of the ship allowed her to slip into oblivion.

Sometime later, when Grace tried to open her eyes, she felt a little strange and was not quite sure where she was or what day it was. She was in a dark room that smelled odd—a salty, sour odour mixed with metal and wood. Her hands felt around her to a strange bed that was most certainly not her own. Her body rocked and swayed against a wave and she sat up suddenly. She was on the wedding ship!

At least her headache appeared to be gone. The room had not been that dark when she'd gone to sleep, she would swear it. How long had she been down there? Whenever this happened at home, sometimes she would not arouse until the next day. Joy knew that. Had she forgotten to wake her?

Squinting in an attempt to get her bearings, she saw there was absolutely no light. As she moved to sit up, the kitten woke and stretched and began attacking her feet.

"Stop that!" she scolded as she swung her legs over the side of the berth and swayed on her feet as they hit the floor. She felt around for her slippers and slid her feet into them. "We must hurry." The wedding party must be over by now, but she could sense the ship was still moving.

She gathered Theodore into her arms and felt for the door before lifting the latch and opening it. It was pitch black in the corridor. She stood there listening for sounds of her family only to be met with silence. There had been too many people present for it to be this quiet. The realization that she must have been left behind sank into her bones. But the ship was moving, she was certain. Had her family yet realized she was gone?

"Oh, no. No, no, no. Surely they would not have left me. There must be some mistake." Mayhap they were only moving the ship somewhere else to dock.

Normally, her bashfulness would have prevented her from going to the deck alone, but her panic at being stranded in the middle of the water overrode her good sense.

Bravely, she decided to climb the steps to the deck and look around, only to find it empty with full darkness overhead, save the moon and stars and a majestic sail taut against the wind. She hurried over to the railing, but they were not close enough to land that she could see it. The boat was cutting swiftly through the water which was not at all good news.

Was there no one about? She may not be an expert, but even she knew that ships did not sail themselves. However, she did not wish to confront the crew alone. Where were they going? To London? Back to Ireland? How long did such a journey take? Ireland was not all that far, but she'd never considered it before. Even though staying inside the small cabin was more appealing than speaking to

ELIZABETH JOHNS

the crew, she must ask them to turn the ship around. If it became public knowledge that she'd been gone unchaperoned overnight, she would be ruined. None of her family would ever divulge such a thing, but secrets had a way of spreading amongst servants and beyond.

She took a deep breath, then turned around to search for whomever was sailing the ship. As she climbed some steps up to what looked like a half deck, she saw the wheel for steering and assumed someone would be there. Strange voices in another language met her ears.

Even though she did not speak any of the Celtic tongues, she deduced it must be the language as Carew's crew was most likely Irish. It held a soothing lyrical tone much like the accent when they spoke English. Interestingly, Carew's English diction was perfect, but she'd heard him slip on occasion.

They still had not noticed her presence. She cleared her throat. "Excuse me, sirs."

"What the devil?" an angry, rough voice asked. She could see by the light of the moon that the voice belonged to a sailor of indeterminate age, whose skin was leathered and wore a thick grizzled beard. The other wore a scarf over his head with bright gold hoops in both of his ears. Was this really a pirate ship?

Grace took a deep breath and steeled herself to speak to these men instead of running in fear back to the cabin. "I seem to have fallen asleep and missed disembarking the ship with the others. Is it possible to turn around and return me?" she asked as politely as she could, doing her best not to appear as intimidated as she felt.

Crude laughter met her request. Why was that funny?

"You've no more chance of that then to squeeze blood from a stone."

"Why not?" she asked, rather than cringe from the crude expression as she struggled to make out the words in the strong-accented brogue.

"Because, lass, we have been sailing for hours. We'd be nowhere near London even if the Captain would agree to take the time to let you off at the nearest port. Which he won't because when he says to make haste, we stop for naught."

"I'd like to speak with the Captain myself." Grace tried to sound more confident than she felt. Whenever Faith spoke that way, people listened.

"Aye, I bet you would. I'm afraid I cannot allow it."

"And why is that?" She was angry enough now at this fellow's impertinence that she forgot to be bashful.

"Because he needs his sleep. He's never to be disturbed unless the ship is about to sink."

"Then I demand to be taken back to London! Surely it would not take so much time to put in at a port and then I may travel back home. If you do it quickly, he will never notice."

This only produced more laughter from the strangers. Why would they not take her seriously? "Maybe you could find your own way," he replied, his voice indicating he thought no such thing, "but the Captain will decide in the morning."

"By then, will we be anywhere near England?"

The man shrugged at her. "It depends on the winds. You could always try swimming, but we're at one of the widest points of the Channel right now."

Even Grace, inexperienced though she was, could tell these men were vastly enjoying toying with her. If only Carew were here. Grace had no idea who the ship's captain was, but she would go and speak with him herself.

"Very well. I will return to my cabin, if that suits you."

One of the men grinned, showing yellow, uneven teeth with a few missing and the other scowled. She turned to leave, grateful that they'd had no inclination to harm her, as Lady Halbury and every chaperone had always prophesied would happen if she dared set foot outdoors alone.

As she turned to go, she paused. She had no idea what to do with the kitten. He must be hungry and need to use the toilet, but she was rather afraid to venture amongst the remainder of the crew below decks.

She turned back. "Pardon me again, sirs, but as you can see, I have a kitten with me. Where may I take him to, to…"

Both of the men glanced at each other, then laughed some more. Ladies did not speak of such things, and they were enjoying her discomfort. She fought tears.

One of them elbowed the other. "The poor mite is going to cry. Here, I'll take care of him."

"Thank you." Grace deposited the kitten into the man's giant paw of a hand then escaped to her cabin. Eventually, the sailor returned Theodore to her, and she shook as she accepted her only companion for what was proving to be the most terrifying thing ever to happen to her.

Grace's panic began to swell like the tide, drowning her as the full weight of her predicament sank in. The implications were too vast and terrible to comprehend fully, yet they came at her in fragments, sharp as shards of glass. Her reputation—what would become of her reputation? An unwed lady, unchaperoned, on a ship overnight, and not just any ship, but one belonging to Lord Carew! Scandal would spread like wildfire, leaping from servant to servant, until the entire *ton* whispered her name in tones of mockery and disdain. She could already hear the murmurs, the snide remarks at assemblies, the titters behind fans. Poor Miss Whitford, so careless as to ruin herself entirely.

Then there was the Captain's refusal to see her. The bluntness of the sailors, their laughter at her expense, echoed in her ears, deepening her helplessness. They had made it plain enough that she was at their mercy, and though they had done her no harm, the uncertainty of their intentions gnawed at her. What sort of man was this captain that his crew should speak of him in such tones? Would he be cold and dismissive, as the sailors had been, or would he be crueller still? She shuddered at the thought, her mind conjuring every grim possibility.

As she curled into herself on the small berth, clutching Theodore to her chest, her thoughts turned dark and frantic. If she could not convince the crew to turn back, what then? How would she explain this to Society? Would the truth even matter, or would her very presence here condemn her irrevocably?

Grace's breath quickened, her chest tightening as panic clawed its way through her. Tears pricked her eyes, hot and unwelcome. She thought of her sisters, of their teasing but loving care. She thought of her home, of the comfort and safety she had taken for granted mere hours ago. How had she allowed this to happen? How had a simple headache led to such a catastrophic turn of events? She allowed herself to sob with frustration and fright until she fell back asleep.

RONAN WAS glad to escape the confines of all the wedded bliss and connubial joy that seemed to accompany his friends and the Whitford sisters of late. They were falling into marriage like a house of cards in rapid succession.

When Ashley Stuart had asked to wed aboard his ship, Ronan could hardly refuse. It did not really put him out, though it delayed his departure a few hours. But now they were finally underway.

The letter he'd received calling him back to Ireland could not have come at a more welcome time. The only bright spot of this trip was being able to participate in catching a criminal—even though his part had been small. There were too few diversions in his life these days.

There was nothing quite like sailing a ship. It was at times like beast versus God and the elements, and at other times gentle and calm. Nothing felt quite like fighting the water, winds and waves and living to tell about it.

Once they had navigated the Thames and the Strait of Dover, he'd relinquished the wheel to O'Brien and escaped to his cabin. Time alone was as essential to him as the very air he breathed. His crew would never bother him unless they needed him to fight a gale.

The peace was welcome because being amongst his friends moving on with their lives had made him realize that things would be different henceforth.

He was not glad for the reason to be called away, however. With his father an invalid and unable to properly protect the family, the task fell to Ronan.

Whenever Ronan was home, Donnagh Flynn left them alone, but as soon as he had word that Ronan had left for England, he would start harassing the family. Flynn meant to get to him through his sister. Unfortunately, he was afraid Maeve would give in to the rogue's charm.

Even though Ronan had taken steps to hide his departure, there was only so much he could do. When his ship was not in the harbour, word eventually got back to Flynn.

Ronan was not certain when the feud between the two families had begun, but it had never ceased since. According to the stories passed down from generation to generation, the Flynn family had always sought to fight the Donnellans for control of the bay that led to the Atlantic, between two peninsulas. There had been one case of romance between the families which had ended in tragedy, akin to Romeo and Juliet. Ronan had no desire to carry on the feud, but neither could he seek reconciliation when Flynn was determined to continue with his nefarious activities. Neither could he allow Maeve to fall into such hands.

Something more permanent would have to be done about the situation, but Ronan did not favour cold-blooded murder, even though Flynn certainly deserved such punishment. It was not the smuggling that bothered Ronan—anyone who'd lived through the rampant poverty from the potato famine not so long ago would never begrudge the only source of income they could find for their families. If that was all he'd done. Ronan shook his head. No, Flynn was known to ruin those who stood in his way. With this on his mind, it was some time before Ronan could fall asleep. His blood boiled any time he thought of Flynn and his touching Maeve that fateful night they'd been introduced, and he'd had the impudence to dance with her before Ronan could stop it.

Whenever they were on board ship, he always woke early so he could watch the sun creep over the horizon. It was an unreal experience that he never tired of. He dressed, left the cabin and climbed up to the quarter-deck, standing at the helm to let the wind rush against his face as the ship cut through the water like a knife.

"*Maidin mhaith*. At this rate, we will be making good time back," Ronan said as he approached O'Brien and Kelly, who'd been at the helm for the night watch. "Any wagers on when we will arrive?"

"No, Cap'n, but there is one small matter you should be aware of." O'Brien was fidgeting nervously, which was odd.

"Shannon deals with small matters," he replied.

"Aye, but Shannon is not with us, if ye recall."

"So he isn't. What is it, then?"

"We have a stowaway. We did not discover them until a few hours ago when we were already well into the Channel. We did not think you would wish us to stop."

Ronan could not think how they had acquired a stowaway. If they'd been in one of the busy ports, perhaps, but they left from Westwood's pier. An ominous sinking feeling came over him, but the two sailors were looking at him with concern.

"Did we do wrong, Cap'n?"

"No. I said we needed to make haste, and we do. But I have a feeling I will not be pleased when I discover who the stowaway is."

"It did seem to be an accident. She demanded to be taken to the closest port immediately," Kelly said by way of a guilty confession.

"And how far is the nearest port now?"

"We're not yet to Portsmouth, but as ye ken, it would be difficult to turn about now."

"Where is she?"

"The first mate's cabin, sir."

Ronan ran his hand over his face. As if matters were not dire enough as it was, now he likely had a Whitford sister on board, whether intentional or accidental, and she had been gone all night. Even if it were possible to sneak her back without anyone knowing, he would be sacrificing precious hours—days, even—to return her, and he'd already delayed enough for the wedding. His sister's fate might already be determined. But if he could save her, then he had to try. Even if he had to sacrifice himself in the process. Westwood was fiercely protective of his wards, and even though he knew Ronan would never harm the girl, her reputation would be in tatters and he would expect Ronan to do the right thing.

"Continue on course. I agree that it's too late to turn about now."

"Aye, aye, Cap'n," O'Brien said with visible relief.

Ronan was furious, but it wasn't his crew's fault. They knew almost as well as he why they were in a hurry.

Delaying the inevitable would not help things, so Ronan decided to go and discover which sister he was to deal with for the near, and possibly forever, future. Was it to be the meek, shy Grace? Or the wild, adventurous, still-in-the-schoolroom Joy? Despite that, he could not envision either one of them stowing away intentionally, but how could such a thing have happened accidentally? One did not just meander off to a secluded part of the ship and remain there for hours until the ship had long sailed. Had she over-imbibed and passed out drunk? Ronan frowned. He had never seen either one of them drink much, if at all. Perhaps seasickness had induced one of them to seek a place to lie down. And how could her family have not noticed she was not with them when they left? Then again, that actually might be more understandable because it had been a bit chaotic and crowded with so many people on deck.

Dread grew with each step he took towards the cabin. Reaching it, he drew a deep breath and hesitated before knocking.

He heard a light thump and then the door was unlocked before Grace Whitford opened it, with her black, glossy hair in a dishevelled mess. Her deep blue eyes widened at the sight of him.

"Lord Carew? I did not expect to see you on board." Her cheeks flushed.

"That makes two of us."

"There has been a dreadful mistake. I had a megrim and was put in here to sleep it off. Then no one woke me. Then I discovered we had sailed in the middle of the night and your crew refused to wake you or turn the ship around or leave me in port." She rambled the words together in one breath. He struggled to keep up then held up his hand to stop her. He had never heard so many words from her mouth.

Often, they'd been paired together the first Season when he had been helping to protect the sisters, but she'd seemed too afraid of him to speak much.

"I realize this was not intentional."

"Then you will take me back?" She looked so hopeful that he hated to disappoint her.

"I am afraid I cannot take you back at this point."

"Why, why not?"

He debated how much to tell her. He needed time to think. "There is an urgent matter I must see to at home. Besides, sailing ships are much at the whim of the tides and winds."

"Oh. I see." She seemed to shrink back into herself. "What will happen to me?"

The way she said it made him burn with anger. Did she really think so little of him that he would just abandon her? Or harm her?

"I cannot yet say. I will have you write a letter to Westwood explaining what happened and I will see it delivered as soon as we reach land. Even if they have already realized you are gone, and are coming after you like the Trojans for Helen, I suspect he trusts me to return you. Which I will, eventually."

"Eventually?" Her voice broke on the word.

"You will be well chaperoned once we arrive. Do try not to look as though I've ruined you in truth. You will come to no harm from me." It was all he could do not to curse his fate right then and there. "I will not keep you prisoner, but I do ask that I accompany you when you go above deck."

A mewling sound came from somewhere within the cabin.

Grace looked back to the berth, then scooped up a little kitten.

"What the devil? We have two stowaways?"

"Joy thought he would comfort me while I slept," she said defensively as she snuggled the cat to her cheek.

It was all Ronan could do not to groan. "I will have breakfast sent to you shortly," he said, then made his escape. This was going to be his most painful voyage yet. What was he to do with a bashful chit and a kitten?

CHAPTER 2

Grace looked around at the small cabin from a new perspective. She was to stay in there, unless Lord Carew decided to escort her on deck? She would go mad! The tiny space could be paced off from end to end in four steps and there was no light or window to see from!

Then he had been short and angry with her, as if she had done it on purpose!

Her own anger grew. He refused to set her down in England, then wished to treat her like a prisoner, regardless of what he said.

Even though she knew her anger was more directed at herself for having fallen asleep and no one remembering to wake her, she still had to vent her frustration, and he was the target before her. He could make things better now, but refused to. He could not turn around, he said. *Would not*, she corrected.

Well, she did not want to stay in the small, dark cabin. Defiance was not a natural inclination for Grace, and her sisters were the only ones who had ever seen such a thing from her, but these were certainly trying circumstances. She felt completely justified in the emotion.

Grace picked up Theodore and cracked open the door for light, then paced back and forth in the tiny space as she deliberated what to do. Only a monster would expect her to stay locked away in this room. As if he would make more than a few minutes here and there to escort her about the ship. He'd been angry, which was a side of him Grace had never seen before. It was frightening, if she were being honest, and made her wonder how much she really knew about him. Had his charming care-for-not façade been just that—an act?

"Begging your pardon, miss," a high-pitched Irish voice cracked from behind as she was on one of her circular routes.

Grace turned to find a freckle-faced, carrot-topped boy of perhaps ten years holding a tray.

"I've your breakfast, miss, if you will follow me."

He kept his head down and did not look at her. How odd. She was allowed to leave the cabin, after all? Surprising, but a small victory. Was there a dining room?

He led her to the door adjacent to hers labelled *Captain*, which opened up into a room thrice the size of her own. Bright windows greeted her on the far wall, while on one side there was a smaller room of sorts that looked to be a bed built into the wall, and on the other side there was a desk and cupboards. A table stood in the centre of the room, which was where he placed her tray.

"There you are, miss. Will you be needing anything else?" he asked nervously, not meeting her gaze. Perhaps he was not often around females.

"Actually, if you could take Theo to wherever cats may do their business, I would be most grateful as I am not supposed to venture out on my own."

The boy's face lit up at the sight of the kitten. He seemed to forget he was shy.

He held out his hands, and he smiled as he took Theo from her. "Aw, you're a little feller, aren't you?"

"Do you know where to take him?" she asked.

He nodded and scratched the kitten's chin. "We have other cats in the hull to keep the mice and rats out. They have a place. I'll make sure and bring him back when he's done."

"Thank you…" She trailed off, hoping he would tell her his name but she very well understood bashfulness and perhaps he needed encouragement. "I am Grace. Do you mind telling me your name?"

Suddenly, he remembered to be afraid of her. "Paddy," he replied, not meeting her eyes.

"Paddy, I am sure he will enjoy a few minutes to stretch his legs and play."

She cast him her biggest smile, hoping at least to have one friend amongst the crew. He was certainly less intimidating than the others she'd met thus far.

Paddy blushed. "Yes, miss," he said, then escaped with Theodore.

Grace tucked into her food. She was more hungry than she cared to admit. It was porridge, which her sisters hated, but she never minded.

"What did you do to that poor boy? He looked moonstruck with a smile as wide as the Atlantic."

Grace stiffened at Carew's voice.

"I did nothing more than greet him and ask him to take Theodore for a turn."

Carew snorted then sat across from her with his own tray.

"A captain retrieves his own meals?"

"Normally, no, but my cabin boy was redirected to another task."

Grace smiled with satisfaction. She'd actually done something a bit naughty. Joy and Patience at least would be so proud.

"That's to be the way of it then?" Carew was looking at her in a new way with one brow raised inquisitively.

She tried not to blush, but was likely unsuccessful. She'd had a bit of an infatuation with him—especially the first Season when he'd been part of their rescuers, as she liked to think of them, and her sisters had teased her maliciously ever since. But who could blame her? Even though he'd shown no interest in her at all, he was a beautiful man. Darkly dangerous with black hair and startling blue eyes, paired with his somewhat secretive and roguish demeanour and—Grace could not explain why she was attracted to such a man. She knew she was too shy and mousy to ever catch someone like him.

Really, it would not be a comfortable match and she appreciated that now. But that never stopped foolish girls from daydreaming, did it? Grace was always bold and beautiful in her dreams.

"You are eating that porridge as if it's your last meal," Carew observed.

"I happen to enjoy porridge, and it is hardly gentlemanly of you to say so."

Carew looked at her with amazement.

"Is something lodged in your throat, my lord?"

"I do not think I've ever heard anyone say they enjoy porridge. The crew complains mightily about it."

"For a time before Lady Halbury took us in, it was the only thing we could afford. I chose to appreciate it instead of the alternative."

He shook his head, then took another bite, still looking a bit perplexed.

Grace finished her bowl and dabbed at her mouth with the napkin provided. It was all rather civilized yet also uncomfortable, eating alone with this man. "Do you normally take meals by yourself?"

"Normally, the first mate joins me. But as you can see, he is not with us this time. His mother was ill and he stayed behind with her."

"I hope she improves." Grace could think of nothing more to say. Now that she had nothing more to eat, she felt awkward sitting in his presence. She'd never been a scintillating conversationalist with anyone except perhaps her sisters, where the wall disappeared that normally surrounded her with strangers. In one aspect, she should be grateful that the Captain was Carew, not someone completely unknown to her. But then again, it had to be Carew who she'd been enamoured of that first Season. Had he realized? In her mind, she'd made an utter fool of herself. With him, she'd either been too tongue-tied to speak, or what she did manage was something stupid and trite.

Part of her was still angry that he would not set her down at the nearest port. But the other sympathetic, rational part of her also understood why he would not. First there was his urgent matter, then there was Westwood. If Carew left her at some strange port and expected her to find her way back, Westwood would be furious. If she'd been stranded with rough sailors, it would've been one thing, but Carew was one of his closest friends.

She would simply have to think of Carew like one of her new brothers. She was not so shy around them, was she? Well, Rotham was very intimidating. She still did not speak much around him.

"How long will the journey take?" she finally asked after she could no longer take the silence.

"A week, give or take."

"Why does it take so long to go to Ireland? It does not look far on the map." She glanced over to the map on the wall above Carew's desk.

"It's over five hundred nautical miles and at five to seven knots per hour, that means it takes nigh seven days."

Grace could only swallow hard. She was to be trapped in that dark, tiny cabin for seven more days? "Be that as it may, I must insist I be allowed to leave the cabin."

"Insist, do you?" He looked amused at Grace's bravery.

She thrust her chin up. "For one, I will need an endless supply of candles. For two, I do not need to be confined like a prisoner. I am very well-behaved."

"Unlike Joy, who I would have expected to find herself in an imbroglio like this."

"Well, yes." No disrespect to Joy, but she did always find herself in scrapes.

"Very well, then. I will allow you to use my cabin during the day so you might have light and more room. The first mate's cabin is normally never used for anything but sleep. However, you may still not venture to the deck without my escort. It is not your behaviour that concerns me."

Grace was not certain what did concern him, then. She knew she should be happy for her small victory, but it was difficult not to rebel at the confinement. "And how often will that be?"

He stood and chucked her under the chin—as if she were a small child!

"Whenever the notion takes me," he said in his deepest Irish brogue, then left. If only she'd had something to throw at him, she would have. So she told her inner bold self.

Ronan chuckled despite himself as he closed the door behind him, his anger dissolving. He'd seen a new and unexpected side of Grace Whitford. Her eyes sparkled and her cheeks took on a bloom that made her dangerously attractive. Apparently all it took to make her forget her meekness was to anger her. Well, he foresaw a great deal of that in the upcoming days. He didn't know if that was good or bad. She would at least be a more entertaining companion, but there was no place in his heart for more than that.

The poor innocent did not understand the likely repercussions of being alone together on a ship with him. He desperately hoped it would not come to her ruination and that Westwood and her family would be able to concoct an eventuality that even the servants would believe. But that would require a miracle, and Ronan did not believe in them. He could not imagine a worse fate than a woman being tied to him in marriage for life, especially someone meek and quiet. He'd done little to earn his roguish reputation, but neither had he ever bothered to dispel it. Perhaps if they could reach land quickly and send word, he and she could escape the parson's noose. Because it would be a noose—for both of them.

If it came to it, he would give her his name, but only his name.

What could he do to keep her content until they reached Ireland? At least there, his mother and sister would be able to take care of her until she could be reunited with her family. Hopefully, Maeve would take to Grace and forget about Flynn…if it wasn't already too late.

Now to pacify his crew, most of whom were waking to this news. He intended to keep her far away from them. Not that he expected any of his men to disobey him or try anything with her. His next point of business was to convince them they were not all doomed because there was a lady on the ship. Most sailors were superstitious as a lot, but to be Irish and a sailor…'twould be nigh impossible to convince them. But he had to try.

He'd already had to bribe Paddy to take a tray to Miss Grace, but since she'd given him the task of helping with the kitten, the boy seemed to have decided she was well enough.

The thought of anyone being afraid of Grace Whitford was laughable. A quieter, sweeter lass than her he'd yet to meet. Perhaps he could draw her out more.

Thank God O'Brien and Kelly had not decided to toss her overboard last night. Apparently, she'd convinced Kelly to take the kitten to relieve himself, which was unbelievable in and of itself. He'd take any small favours at the moment.

Most hands were on deck going about their morning chores as he gained the quarter-deck. They were a rough lot, his crew—a patchwork of hardened, weathered faces each carrying the marks of hard work. There was Murphy, the grizzled boatswain with a voice that could be heard even in the fiercest squall, his tangled beard streaked with grey and his nose permanently reddened by years of rum and biting winds. O'Brien, his second mate, with an uncanny ability to spot danger long before it appeared, had a lined, weathered face from years in the elements. Then there was Kelly, the quiet navigator whose shoulders were broad from years of breaking horses.

As he surveyed the scene, he wondered what Grace had made of them when she'd awoken and encountered them alone last night. He imagined her taking in the rough edges and gruff demeanours with fear. The crew was a far cry from the refined gentlemen to which she was accustomed in Mayfair. These men had bawdy ways, and their manners were non-existent.

He could almost see her now, standing at the edge of the deck last night, her gloved hands clasped in front of her as she tried to reconcile the tales she'd read of pirates in her novels with the reality before her. How out of place she must have felt when she first stepped aboard his ship, surrounded by these rough, coarse men.

"The weather's a-changin'. I can feel it in me bones," Kelly prophesied.

"Of all the times to need good weather, this is it," Ronan said.

"You should drop the chit at Portsmouth or Plymouth," O'Brien warned.

"The ship is not cursed because she is on board. That is an old wives' tale. And you know why I cannot take the time to do it. Besides being the ward of one of my closest friends, who would run me through if I did such a thing, I cannot give Flynn any further time. He does not think I will make it back by Samhain."

O'Brien cast him a scathing look then crossed himself. If anyone else had tried that, Ronan would've flogged him, but O'Brien was like a second father to him and had been with him since he was a lad.

"Where did the superstition come from, that having a female on a ship curses it?" he wondered aloud, though he'd heard it his whole life.

"All I know is that women distract the crew, which angers the sea goddess, causing her to send the waters into tumult." O'Brien shuddered.

"Clearly, that is the case," Ronan pointed out dryly.

"If only you'd make some effort to appease the goddess, Cap'n," O'Brien chastised.

That appeasement being ever so convenient for the male crew. Tale had it that naked women calmed the sea, which is why so many figureheads were unclothed creatures. The figurehead of *The Selkie* was the mythical creature herself, half-seal, half-human.

But Ronan did agree something was in the air and he only prayed it was stronger winds to take them home faster.

Ronan spoke up. "Gather around." His crew came to stand at the edge of the quarter-deck, and he looked down upon them with O'Brien and Kelly alongside, about to go to their berths to sleep. They were rough enough that they tended to stay below decks when other people were around, hence the night watch.

"As you've no doubt heard by now, we have an unexpected visitor on board. I want no one to go near her without my permission. I also want no one to speak of her or of being cursed by her. She will be treated with courtesy when you see her. She is under my protection and anyone who disobeys will answer to me. Is that understood?"

"Aye, aye, Captain."

Well, if they did not say it with any gusto, they could not be blamed. He dismissed everyone then rechecked their course. The winds were steady, they were moving along at five knots and thus far not a cloud in the sky. He locked the wheel with the helm line, then stood back and watched the sea.

What was he going to do with Grace Whitford when they arrived? He would be too occupied with Flynn and whatever damage he decided to inflict on Ronan's family this time to worry about her.

The problem of Flynn needed a permanent solution. This feud could not continue any longer. Especially not with Maeve caught in the middle—like the knot in a tug-of-war. Theories of its origin ranged from thwarted young love to jealousy over King Henry III's favour.

At one time, Ronan had truly believed there was hope for a friendly generation. Why should something centuries old, that no one really knew the cause of, affect them now?

As young boys, they had befriended each other at school before either realized who the other was or why it mattered. Once the amity was discovered, it was quickly snuffed out and the vitriol infused into this generation by Flynn's father, Baron Corlach. It was as though new life had been breathed into the feud.

Flynn had begun to terrorize and attack Ronan, which admittedly taught him to fight. Ronan had been sent to England to school after that, which was only a temporary reprieve. However, he'd made powerful friends, and it might be he would have to call in a favour from them to save his sister.

Flynn's attacks had escalated with each passing year, his hostility against the Donnellan clan seeming to fester like an untreated wound. At first, it had been petty things—spreading false rumours, tampering with crops, and stirring unrest among the tenants. Ronan had confronted Flynn on numerous occasions, but words had proved futile. All the while, Flynn's twisted charm masked the malice that lay beneath.

When Flynn began encroaching on Donnellan land, it became a

more direct affront. Fences were torn down, livestock went missing, and fields were set ablaze under the cover of night. Ronan had tried to rally the local magistrates, but Flynn's cunning ensured there was never enough evidence to hold him accountable. And then there was the poisoning of Donnellan's prized horses—an unforgivable act.

Then he'd begun trying to control the waters. Flynn had turned to piracy, seizing merchant vessels and demanding bribes for safe passage. Ronan had armed his crew and patrolled the bay himself, but Flynn's network of informants always seemed one step ahead. The losses mounted, and the locals suffered, further entrenching the hatred between their families.

It had been one thing for Flynn to terrorize the bay and seas of Ireland like the pirate he was, but now to threaten Ronan's sister?

That was beyond anything Ronan could tolerate. Flynn's audacity had crossed a line. It was no longer about revenge; it was about survival...and protecting those Ronan held most dear.

He wished his mother had been more specific about the threat so Ronan could prepare his strategy. She'd only said, "Come quickly, Maeve is falling into his clutches." What did that mean? Ronan was afraid he knew.

Flynn had made it his life's mission to destroy the Donnellans, and it was Ronan's to stop him.

CHAPTER 3

Meanwhile, back at Taywards...

"When was the last time anyone saw Grace?" Westwood asked the group as they stood around after the wedding, ready to climb into carriages to depart for London.

"She was not feeling well during the wedding breakfast this morning, so I sent her to a cabin to lie down," Faith explained.

"She must have fallen asleep," Patience said with dawning realization.

All of the sisters exchanged panicked glances. Grace could sleep through the second coming.

"Oh, no!" Faith's hand flew to her mouth. "We must return to the docks to see if we can catch them before they sail."

"Ashley and I will go. The rest of you can go on to London, if you wish, before darkness falls," Westwood said.

Patience could sense the hesitance, but Rotham took charge. "Even if she is on that ship, there is little for any of us to do. Carew will bring her back."

Patience did not wait to see what the others decided. She was not about to be left behind. She ran to the stables and helped saddle another horse before they all set off towards the docks.

As they dismounted from their mounts, tied them to posts and ran out on the pier, they all stopped, their breaths heaving. There was no ship there.

"We are too late." Patience stated the obvious as Westwood uttered a curse.

"Do we follow after them?" Ashley asked.

"No," Patience answered. "What is done is done."

"Carew will bring her back unharmed," Westwood said with conviction.

Yet none of them asked the question that was heavy on all of their minds. What would happen to her reputation? There was no secret that Grace was enamoured with the Irish Earl, but he'd shown her no more attention than mere solicitousness. Not the type of connection anyone would want for their sister, Patience mused, especially not now that three of them had found true love.

They stood there staring at the water, as if they could beckon Carew's ship back by sheer will alone.

"The tide is strong, and who knows how long it will be until he even realizes she is a stowaway?" Ashley asked.

"She did not do it on purpose." Of that, Patience was certain. Grace was not bold enough nor confident enough in her feminine wiles ever to do such a thing.

"I trust him implicitly," Westwood said with a hand on her shoulder.

Patience nodded. It was of little comfort to know Grace's fate was out of their hands.

As they returned to deliver the news to the others, the news was not well received.

"What do you mean Grace is gone?" Faith asked, even though she had to know well and good what had happened.

"I mean that she is not here."

"Are we ready to depart?" Hope asked as she came into the room. She stopped when she saw Faith. "Is something the matter?"

"Grace did not come off the ship," Joy explained.

"Then someone should go and fetch her. If we do not set out for London soon, it will be too late to go today."

"The ship is gone, Hope. It sailed immediately after the wedding."

"Oh, dear," Hope said faintly as she sat next to Faith and took her hand for comfort.

"What do we really know of Carew?" Faith asked.

"He is a deliciously mysterious Irishman?" Hope offered.

Rotham scoffed.

Faith ignored the remark. "I have never been concerned about him because he is your friend, but you must admit he does not have the best reputation," she said to Westwood.

"He has shown no interest in Grace, even though she was taken with him," Joy said unhelpfully and received a reprimanding look from her sisters. "It is true."

"Carew will not harm her," Westwood said emphatically.

"I am relieved to hear it, but that only matters to us. Once word gets out, she will be ruined and we all know it. The servants are probably already talking about it."

"Then we must control the damage at once." He opened the door and called for Hartley. Rotham strode into the room, dressed in buckskins, a many-caped greatcoat, and Hessians for travel.

"You must speak not a word to your servants, and carry on to London as you were. We will say Grace went with you, and you will say Grace stayed with us. That should delay discovery until we hear from Carew as to when and where to fetch her."

"You cannot think to leave her all alone with those, those sailors!" Faith spat the word as though it were venom.

"I feel for Grace, truly I do, but what good would it do to chase after them at this point?"

"We would have our Grace back far more quickly?" she answered rhetorically. "We have no idea what state she is in!"

"But we cannot be certain of the route he is taking. It would only delay a satisfactory reunion by chasing all over who knows where. And I am not a sailor." Westwood threw up his hands.

"How many routes are there to Ireland? You do know where he lives, do you not?" she retorted.

"I thought it had been decided that we will wait for Carew to return her," Rotham remarked.

"My lord?" the butler enquired as he stepped into the room.

"Hartley, there was some confusion as to where Miss Grace was. If you hear anyone speak about her being missing, please reassure them that we know exactly where she is. I do not wish to hear any gossip otherwise."

"Yes, my lord."

After the butler had closed the door behind him, Faith turned back to Westwood. "Dominic Stuart, we will go after my sister at once. If you refuse to help, then I will go by myself and take whoever cares to come with me."

"Carew will take care of her."

"That will do little to salvage her reputation, sir. A chaperone is what my sister needs at the moment."

"I cannot like you going anywhere since you recently gave birth. Think of the baby," Westwood said softly.

"Nor you," Rotham said to Hope.

"I would love to go, and Freddy can go with me," Joy remarked, and several looks were cast her way. "She would not be alone, at least, and I did not just give birth," Joy pointed out the obvious, of course not thinking of Freddy Cunningham as an eligible bachelor.

"But you would be alone until you joined her," Faith said.

"You are game to come along, are you not?" She nudged her friend in his side.

"Of course." Mr. Cunningham agreed as he always did.

Personally, it seemed very reasonable to Patience, and though she would never say it, she didn't think Faith was completely rational since having the baby.

"Mayhap Major Stuart and Patience would be better suited for such a task. They would fit both rescuer and chaperone," Hope suggested.

"But they are just married," Faith argued.

Patience and Ashley exchanged glances. She did not mind if he did not.

"We will go," Ashley offered.

"Excellent. We have a plan. I will see to it," Rotham said, trying to urge everyone out of the door. "I will send another rider to alert my crew to ready my yacht. It is not as big as Carew's ship, but may catch them faster."

"I am most grateful to you," Westwood said and quickly shook Rotham's hand before the party exited the house.

As the others took their leave, the entry hall and drive buzzed with a flurry of purpose. Instructions were exchanged in clipped tones, and the gentlemen and servants moved determinedly, their urgency tangible. As the others drove away from the house, Faith lingered with worry.

She touched Westwood's arm lightly. "Stay a moment," she murmured, her voice steady but low enough to keep their conversation private. Westwood's brows furrowed, but he nodded and closed the door softly behind him. He gestured for her to speak.

"We must discuss what happens should this situation come to light," she began, her tone practical. "Whilst I am relieved there is a plan to retrieve Grace, we cannot ignore the consequences should even a whisper of this reach Society. Her prospects, her reputation… everything hangs in the balance."

Westwood exhaled heavily, rubbing a hand over his face. "I've already spoken to Hartley. He will quell any rumours amongst the servants. Ashley and Patience will track her down. We will tell everyone she was with family the entire time."

Westwood did not seem to understand the gravity of Grace's situation.

"Even if Grace returns safely, she is with Carew…"

"Indeed. Whilst I do not think he will harm her, I cannot see him as a good match for Grace. Two more incompatible beings would be difficult to find. There is a darkness to him that I would shield her from."

"Then we must consider the possibility of a swift marriage to someone else."

Westwood's brows lifted, and a wry smile curved his lips. "And would you have a candidate in mind, my lady? Or do you intend for me to scour the countryside?"

"I trust you would find no shortage of eager suitors," Faith replied lightly, "but I would suggest we tread carefully. Any arrangement must be for Grace's happiness as well as her reputation."

Westwood nodded with resolution. "I will consider it, but she has had plenty of time to choose someone else and has not."

CHAPTER 4

Now, being cooped up in a cabin like this, Grace did not mind. Would she have appreciated it had she not experienced the other? She liked to think she would as she was often wont to steal away to a secluded corner to read at home.

It looked much like a man's study, walls panelled with wood, windows and space to walk around, and most importantly, there was a shelf of books. That should occupy her for most of the week, and no one would disturb her.

A knock on the door interrupted her perusal of book titles for her reading pleasure.

"Enter," she called, though she had no idea if she should be answering the door to Lord Carew's cabin.

It was Paddy with Theodore. Grace smiled. "Did he enjoy his time with the other cats?"

"Hard to say, miss. One of them hissed something fierce, but they always do that when there's someone new. The other one seemed to take to him just fine."

"Thank you for helping me with him."

"It's no trouble, miss. It's better than some of my duties, which the Cap'n says I need to return to now." He looked over at the trays, then went to stack the dishes and proceeded to carry them away. "I will come back for 'im when I bring the midday meal," the boy said wistfully.

"Until then." She waved, then turned back to the surprising collection of novels. It was another unexpected facet to Carew. Many of them she had read before, but she never minded re-reading them. There was always some new detail she had missed the time before that would delight her.

"Oh! *Frankenstein!*" But when she pulled the first volume from the shelf, it was brand new and had not yet been cut. She inhaled the scent with the awe and wonder the new leather deserved.

"That's wholly disappointing though," she said to no one in particular. She would not ask to christen the book herself, though it would kill her not to read it. But she could never be so bold. Mayhap it was a gift for the sister he had mentioned, or his mother.

Instead, she selected one of the Radcliffe novels, then looked around for where to sit. There was the table with benches that were nailed to the floor, the bed tucked into an alcove in the wall that she dared not touch. It must belong to the Captain and 'twould be far too intimate. There was a narrow seat beneath the window that was just wide enough for her. "That will have to do. In fact, it looks like it was made for this very thing."

Theodore was exploring the new environs, and she left him to it. "This is much, much better, is it not?" she said to him, though he only responded by pouncing on something Grace could not see. Perhaps she could find something to fashion a toy for him. Joy was always making things to entertain Freddy and now the kittens, so perhaps Paddy could help her find something for Theo.

Grace kicked off her slippers and climbed onto the seat, and for a while, became distracted by the view. Before the wedding, she'd never been on a sailing ship or the sea and never before where she couldn't see land at all. There was water as far as the eye could see.

Birds were gliding out over the open water, then would swoop down and come up with a fish in their mouths. This made her contemplate the majesty of Creation and the circle of life. She never really liked to think about the fact that some animals ate others to survive, which always led her to examine her own diet, which was laden with meat. She could not think on it. Now she needed a distraction.

If she weren't so concerned about what would happen to her or how her family must be worrying, she might take a bit more enjoyment in this adventure, but hers was not an adventurous spirit.

Even though she was never one to hold a grudge, she was entitled to be upset about this situation. First, her family had forgotten about her—namely Joy. Then she was surprisingly angry at Carew, and her anger made her shockingly bold. Faith had been bold because she'd had to be. Patience was both bold and adventurous. Grace was more like Hope, except Hope had always wanted a grand marriage and now she had it. What did Grace want? Happiness, peace, tranquillity? Love? Of course she wanted to be loved, but that was a vague notion, and it was difficult to place a finger on what she wanted.

As she opened the book and began to read, Grace smiled when she read the name Theodore. Joy loved Miss Radcliffe's books, very likely because her governess had read them to her while she was recovering from her injury. She had named each of the kittens for her respective heroes and heroines.

Theodore was not particularly the sharpest, smartest hero, nor did he win the heroine in the end, but he still had some redeeming qualities. Time would tell if the nomenclature fit the little feline. Thus far, he was quite adorable and cuddly.

"I would not mind my own hero with such qualities," she mused. None of Radcliffe's heroes particularly appealed to Grace, but the stories were entertaining, nonetheless.

She became so lost in the story that she did not notice the hours pass, and the knock on the door surprised her.

Jumping to her feet, she attempted to straighten herself as best she could. It was only the cabin boy with an afternoon meal.

"Afternoon, miss," Paddy said as he entered the room and set down the tray. His eyes immediately searched the cabin for Theo, who was sleeping on the bench, stretched out on his back like he had not a care in the world.

"You may pet him if you like," Grace encouraged. She could only imagine this young boy did not have many small pleasures, working as he did.

He smiled shyly, then crept gingerly over to the cat, as if anything would wake him.

"How are things on deck?" she asked, curious for some hints of life outside the cabin. She had heard various bumps, creaks, and voices, but had no idea what or who they belonged to.

"Nothing special. Just the usual, though the quartermaster says the weather is a-changin'."

"How so? Is there going to be a storm?" Her eyes darted to the window and she could see a few clouds forming, but that was not so unusual for an afternoon in England. If they were even near England. She assumed Ireland's weather was much the same, but perhaps it was different on the sea.

"I'm not certain, but I trust the quartermaster. He can feel it in his bones, 'e says. 'E's been on a ship his whole life."

Grace nodded because she was unsure of what to say to that. One of their old retainers back at Halbury Hall had predicted cold weather in much the same way.

"What happens if there is a storm?"

The boy shrugged as he stroked Theodore's fur. "Depends. Sometimes they make me go below if it's bad enough."

The thought of the rough crew caring enough about this young boy to ensure his safety warmed her heart. Perhaps they were not so bad after all, even if the sight of them did scare her.

"Do you like to read a lot?" He pointed to the book she had left on the seat.

"It is one of my favourite things in the world."

"The Cap'n makes us learn our letters, me and Barry. That and we 'ave—have—to learn to speak English proper."

Grace smiled as he struggled with his aitches. She assumed Barry was another young boy. She did not know why Carew's insistence on education should surprise her so much, but it did. It was not common for the lower classes to read or write, but Westwood also did the same with his servants.

"He says it will give us better 'tunities later."

Grace smiled at the boy's efforts to use the big word. "Indeed, I believe he is correct in that."

"I best get back to my duties," he said with a heavy sigh.

As he turned to leave, Grace remembered something. "Paddy, would you see if you can find me a stick, a piece of string about this long," she held her arms out wide, "and perhaps a feather?"

The boy looked at her as if she were daft before remembering himself. Then she could see him trying to think of where to find those things. "I think I can. The string will be the easiest," he remarked, and then seemed to hurry away with excitement.

Grace laughed as she set to her meal of a simple stew with bread. The boy's exuberance reminded her of Joy.

RONAN WATCHED the quickly changing skies and cursed. He'd intended to bring Miss Grace on deck so she could have some fresh air and stretch her legs, and now there was not much time. He turned and hurried towards his cabin, which was odd in and of itself because he never hurried anywhere.

He opened the door without knocking because, well, it was his cabin and he could not imagine Grace Whitford doing anything in there he'd need to knock for.

It took him a moment to find her, but she was sleeping on the narrow window seat, book open on her chest and the kitten in the bend of her legs. It was a rather charming scene if one were in the mood to be charmed. Ronan was not.

"What am I to do with you, Grace Whitford?" he murmured. His normal inclination was to flirt and tease women, which he meant absolutely nothing by. For some reason, Grace did not inspire flirtatious behaviour in him, though he could not say why. Although now that he knew what it was to anger her, the devil in him would very likely stoke that fire within her.

He stroked a finger down her cheek in an attempt to wake her, which was also playing with fire, but that porcelain skin was much too tempting to resist. She started a little, but did not wake. He bent over and began to whisper nonsensical Irish in her ear. Her face turned towards him, bringing their noses within an inch of each other, then her eyes opened wide.

They watched each other for a moment, blue eyes to blue, before she finally asked. "What are you doing?"

"I was trying to wake you."

She set the book aside, then sat up and, gloriously dishevelled, moved the cat from her lap.

"To what purpose?"

"To escort you above deck before the weather changes."

Apparently, that was the correct answer, for she smiled at him and slipped her feet into the dainty little slippers that women used as an excuse for footwear.

She stood too quickly and wobbled, then the boat lurched and threw her into the table. He only partially caught her, softening the landing a little. The feel of her in his arms was a bit too tempting for his own comfort. She was certainly more luscious than he would have expected by her slim frame, and the faint scent of lilacs about her was strangely alluring on her.

Thankfully, she seemed unmoved, and wholly unaware of his wayward thoughts, which was a very, very good thing.

Promptly, he helped her stand upright. "It takes a while to find your sea legs."

"Sea legs?"

"Learning to find your balance while the floor moves beneath you. About the time you get used to it, we will be on land and then that will feel strange for a few days."

Ronan led her through the door to the companionway, then up the ladder to the main deck. Unfortunately, the sky had grown much darker since he'd gone to the cabin.

"It smells like rain," she said as she held on to the shroud and looked up at the sky.

Ronan had always thought the weather had a smell himself, and had been teased by his sister about it. He was somehow pleased that she thought the same.

"It will rain and hopefully that is all. If you notice, the sails are not full. The wind has stilled and that means we may stop moving."

Her brow furrowed, then she walked over to the railing and seemed to contemplate his words for a few moments. "Does water ever truly stop moving?"

"Actually, no, but the wind does. We are going against the current, so if there is no wind to harness, we essentially stop."

"Or get carried backwards by the current?" she asked perceptively.

"We have ways to stop from going backwards, but unfortunately, until the wind picks up, we cannot go forward."

"How do you sail against the wind?"

"By tacking. You must sail at an angle, then change to the opposite angle then so on and so forth, essentially to go in the direction you wish."

"Fascinating. I had never really thought about it before."

"I do not suppose you would have had cause to."

She humphed grumpily. "Ladies rarely have need to do anything, do they?"

It was hard for him not to smile at her peevishness. Had she always been like this and he had simply never looked? He glanced at her with reluctant appreciation. No, she'd been hiding this side of herself, he was sure of it. Either that or she'd been afraid of him before and no longer was. He was not certain that was a good thing either.

He was pleased by her keen mind. She'd never carried on much conversation with him before. He had not thought her slow, precisely, but had thought she was one of the young, mindless chits that London Society seemed to cultivate.

"What is this?" She climbed up to the quarter-deck and explored while Fergus eyed her warily. Hopefully, Grace did not notice how all of the men were giving her a wide berth. At least no one had spat and crossed themselves where she could see.

There was a loud crack of thunder and the skies opened in a downpour and he hurried her back down the ladder to the cabin. She stopped suddenly in front of him and he barely kept from stumbling into her.

"Oh! I left Theodore up there!"

"Theodore? You mean the cat? It is named Theodore?" he asked scathingly. "What a ridiculous name for a cat."

"Joy," she remarked by way of explanation, but was already hurrying past him back up to the deck.

Ronan looked skyward, then followed her. The last thing he wished to do was drown in the rain over a rat catcher. He'd left Fergus watching the wheel—not that they were going anywhere—and he was protected from the rain by his oilskin. Chasing a kitten was not calling to him as staying warm and dry in the cabin was.

When they reached the deck, the rain was coming down in heavy sheets that splashed in puddles.

From what he knew of cats, they were self-serving creatures. The kitten was likely smart enough to be hiding somewhere and would not come out until the rain stopped, but Ronan could tell any mention of that fact would fall on deaf ears when he saw Grace searching frantically. She did not even know the ship well enough to search, and the crew was already sour, blaming her for the rain and the lack of wind. It was convenient to forget all of these things happened when she was not on board as well.

In a mood himself, he went to the most likely places for a small rat-sized creature to hide and found him curled up in the middle of a rope, dry underneath an overhang. He scooped the kitten up in his hand and shoved him inside his waistcoat before calling out to Grace. "I have him."

Speaking of rats, she looked like a drowning one. He took her by the elbow and hurried her back towards the companionway and down to the cabin. He closed the door behind him, then pulled the little feline out of his coat and held him out for her inspection.

"How is he dry?"

"He was napping, blissfully unaware beneath an overhang."

Suddenly aware that they were both dripping puddles on his rug, he went to the cupboard and began pulling dry clothing out for himself and a flannel for her to wrap herself in.

"Pardon me, but I will go and change in another cabin."

When he returned, she was still standing there, shivering, wrapped in the flannel he'd given her. She had removed her slippers and put them somewhere to dry, he supposed, but then he cursed himself.

"You have no change of clothes, do you?"

She shook her head as though ashamed. This was going to be a very long week. He went back to the cupboard, desperately searching for something she could change into. He'd never had a female on board for an overnight stay. Occasionally, Maeve would sail with him, but it was always around the bay and back.

If only he had brought her with him this time how different everything might be.

He came back from the cupboard empty-handed. "Let me see if one of the boys has something that might fit you. You may remove your wet things. I promise not to intrude when I return, but you cannot remain like that or you will catch a chill." He did not wait for her answer but escaped through the door.

CHAPTER 5

Grace watched the door for a few moments after Lord Carew left through it, as if it would give her answers. She was frozen into immobility by the chill and the thought of undressing in his cabin, but what he said was reasonable. No one could see in the windows in the middle of the Channel, and she could not stand there and freeze to death.

She pulled her wet clothing off as best she could, grateful that the dress she'd worn that day was practical enough not to need a maid.

She re-wrapped herself in the other side of the flannel that was mostly dry and waited for him to return. When he did, he knocked on the door, then opened it a crack to shove some clothing through.

"I'm sorry it is not a dress, but these clothes will have to do for now. At least they are dry," he said through the door.

"True enough. Thank you."

When she made to close the door, he held it open.

"Hand me your wet clothes. We have a place to dry them near the fire in the kitchen."

She hesitated.

"No one will see your undergarments, lass," he said rather softly, understanding her reluctance. "It will take ten times as long to dry here in this cabin and you'll be in the boy's clothing longer."

She knew he was right, but it did not make it any less mortifying.

"Very well." She handed him her sopping wet clothing balled up, then quickly put on the rough cotton shirt, breeches, and stockings. She felt ridiculous and even a bit scandalous with no shift for modesty. She would just have to keep the flannel about her.

Lord Carew returned much too quickly, and she wondered if she should go back to her small cabin. But the thought of being cooped up in that dark room was about as appealing as eating raw turnips.

"Would you like me to return to my cabin?" she asked, thinking it wasn't really her decision to make.

"I thought we could play cards or chess, unless you wish to return to your story." He angled his head towards the book, which lay closed on the bench.

"You do have a rather nice selection of novels."

"It helps pass the time. I buy them for my sister, then I also read them so I know what she's talking about. They are amusing, mostly, if not ridiculous."

"I love escaping into stories and imagining that I am in another place," she admitted, and then blushed, realizing how freely she'd spoken.

"I can understand that. Sometimes I'd like to go beyond England and Ireland. But for now, it is not possible."

"Is your sister in danger?" She watched him closely as he narrowed his gaze.

"Aye."

Grace nodded and whispered, "I am truly sorry. I never meant to add to your worries."

"'Tis quite a predicament we are in. I know you did not stow away on purpose, but I hope you understand why I cannot afford the time to take you back."

"What kind of danger is she in, your sister?"

Lord Carew pointed to one of the benches at the table and she sat down. He pulled a chess set from a shelf and set it on the table then sat down himself.

"I am not very good," she warned.

He shrugged. "It passes the time." He waved his hand for her to go first, and she moved her white queen pawn forward.

He raised his brow at what must have been an amateur move, then moved his own king knight. "For centuries, there has been a feud between the families of Flynn and Donnellan."

She moved another pawn, allowing him to tell the story.

"Both families live on Kenmare Bay, one to the north and one to the south. Naturally, both families believe they own the bay. It provides access to the Atlantic as well as towards England and the Continent."

Grace looked up. "They cannot share?" As the fourth of five sisters, sharing had been ingrained in her very early on. His look made her feel as though she could not understand.

"It would be too easy to share."

She looked at him with astonishment.

He held a pawn up in his hand. "'Tis the way of things, lass. Control of land and water is power."

She had to confess, the way he said lass was enchanting. He seemed to forget to use proper English diction once he left its shores. She rather liked the Irish lilt.

"So they have always fought?"

"The stories go back for many generations at least."

"So there is some kind of trouble now?"

"The son of the current baron is a scoundrel. He has threatened to make off with my sister if I do not return and negotiate by Samhain."

"The pagan holiday?"

"Very fitting, is it not?" He scowled. "He can only make these threats when I am away."

"Does your sister know?"

Carew growled deep in his throat. "Oh, yes. But she is completely taken with him."

"How was she able to know him if your families hate each other? Would you not avoid each other?"

"Normally that was the case. People knew better than to invite both families to the same events. However, the region is small, and at times it could not be avoided, such as the end of harvest festival. I had escorted Maeve there, and she ran off with friends. The next thing I knew, she was dancing with the blackguard."

"Did she know who he was?"

"Aye, but Maeve thought she could convince him to see the error of his ways—end the feud with friendship. Flynn is also a handsome devil at that." His lips twisted sardonically, as though he was not the most handsome man she'd ever seen himself.

"What did Maeve say afterwards?"

"That it was just a dance, and not to worry myself. I should have known that would not be the end of it."

Grace gasped. "You mean she would go willingly?"

"She is young and doesn't understand he means to get to me through her. She is deceived by a pair of beautiful green eyes and a serpent's tongue."

Grace could understand that as she looked into a pair of fathomless deep blue ones.

"But what kind of man takes his bride in such a way? She gets nothing out of it but him. If he actually means to marry her. He's not above ruining her. It's more what I'd expect."

"He sounds worse than a scoundrel!" Grace exclaimed in mortification.

"He waits until I am away since my father is not strong enough to protect the family. My poor mother is beside herself."

Grace felt for him. All this time she had known him, she had never known any of this about him, having only ever thought of him as the care-for-naught people described him as. Was it all an act? She did not know him very well at all, she realized. "Is your sister of an age to choose him for herself?"

"Almost, and Flynn knows it. Her birthday is just past Samhain and I must get there in time to convince her it would be a horrible mistake. I would rather give in to his demands than see my sister bound to him in misery for life."

"What are his demands?"

"The rights to Kenmare Bay."

"Show me where it is." Grace rose from the table and walked over to the map on the wall. She tried not to watch as he rolled up his sleeves, and busied herself finding Ireland and studying it more closely than she ever had before. He leaned over her and pointed to a finger-like projection. This is the Kenmare Peninsula, which is my family's land. This is Flynn's land." He pointed to another area of land that jutted out from the main island.

"So this bay in between is what he wants control of?" She barely managed to speak because his nearness was disconcerting her.

"Yes." He stepped back and she was able to breathe.

Carew returned to the table and waited for her to come back before sitting. Grace glanced at the map once more, thinking she would study it better once he was gone. There were so many questions she wished to ask, but he seemed disinclined to explain further. She could, however, discern that whatever conflict lay between him and this Flynn fellow, it had deeply affected him.

Carew moved his knight, capturing her bishop with a deft slide of the piece across the board.

Grace bit her lip, staring at the board. She knew she was going to lose; it was becoming increasingly clear as she struggled to decide her next move. Even a distracted Carew revealed a much keener mind than she had anticipated. She supposed she didn't mind losing to him, though.

As she pondered her predicament, her thoughts wandered. She marvelled at how she could feel so drawn to someone with such a rakish reputation—something that should have repulsed her entirely. Perhaps it had been his beauty that captivated her from afar, but proximity to him only heightened her awareness of her own inadequacies. Yet here, forced together on this voyage, her reticence was slipping away, and she was unsure whether that was a good or a dangerous thing. After all, he had evidenced none of the rakish behaviours she had so feared—at least, not aboard this ship.

Without fully thinking it through, she nudged a pawn forward. Carew's eyebrow arched, and his lips curled into that wry smile she was beginning to recognize.

Was she mistaken, or was there a new warmth in his eyes? The realization made her heart pound uncomfortably. She forced her gaze back to the board.

"Checkmate," he pronounced, sliding his queen into position, cutting off her king's escape.

She laughed, despite herself. "Defeated."

"Indeed," he said, standing and grabbing the oilskin coat draped over the back of the door. "I should go and see how Fergus does." He sounded almost hurried, as though eager to escape, and left before she could respond.

Grace sighed and leaned back in her chair. She reached over to stroke Theo. The kitten had made himself at home on the edge of the table. "I must have been mistaken, Theo," she murmured softly. But her heart still fluttered, betraying her uncertainty.

~

RONAN HAD to get out of this cabin. This new Grace was unexpected and uncomfortable. No, in fact, he wasn't uncomfortable, which was the problem. He was enjoying her company, which made him uncomfortable.

He'd never thought twice about this timid Whitford sister before, but he'd never taken the time to look. She was much of an age with his sister, but it was not that so much as he'd always been attracted to a confident, outspoken sort of woman. More like her elder sister, though that had never been a serious interest. The devil inside him had enjoyed toying with Westwood.

So what was wrong with him now? It was inexplicable. Beautiful women threw themselves at him all the time, and he was not even being arrogant about it. He wasn't an eyesore and he held a title, even if it was an Irish one. What was special about Grace Whitford to make him feel this way? He must be coming down with something.

He'd found himself talking about his feud with Flynn, which he never spoke of to anyone save his family. Then he'd had to stop himself as they studied the map. Something about her had drawn him dangerously close, and he began envisioning things that were not entirely wholesome. He had caught himself just in time. Grace Whitford deserved better than him, but he was becoming more and more concerned that he was precisely who she was going to get—like it or not.

He was also becoming more and more certain that this feud with Flynn would be a fight to the death. The last time he had tried reasoning with Flynn, the man had laughed in his face.

It would be hard for Grace if she was to become too attached. She'd have his name, and then be free.

More concerning was what would become of Maeve, who was the innocent pawn in all of this nonsense. He'd love nothing better than to put an end to all of it for good. Except Flynn was determined to ruin his family's honour one way or another, which left Ronan no choice.

As he climbed on deck, he welcomed the rain in his face. He relieved Fergus from the wheel and contemplated what was next. If this was to be his lot, then he would face it bow to the wind. Although, ironically, the bow was facing the non-existent wind at the moment and they were literally going nowhere. The rain was coming straight down, indicating that the storm was not going to be blowing away soon. The Channel weather was notoriously fickle, but rarely dead still. Ronan needed his luck to change and quickly. This could not be a foreshadowing of what was to come. He could not allow himself to think that way.

Ronan leaned forward over his hands, resting across the railing, feeling the weight of the world on his shoulders and allowing a moment of self-pity. He knew he could not indulge for long and needed to use his energies to form a plan, but sometimes it was just too much.

He slammed his fist down on the helm impatiently. He needed to be doing something useful, and the cursed ship could not even be sailing to help. They could be stuck for days, but he did not think it likely. Calm and rational was what he needed to remain, but he'd heard stories of ships being caught in the doldrums for weeks. God knew what would become of his sister and family if that happened. He prayed earnestly for wind to set them moving again, and that Westwood would come to fetch his sister-in-law before her fate was disastrously set with Ronan himself.

"Captain?"

Ronan stood straight and turned around. He had not heard Fergus approach.

"What is it, mate?"

It must be important for Fergus to return so soon after he'd been relieved from the wheel. His eyes shifted nervously.

"Speak, man. What is it?"

"The men are agitated."

"About what?" Ronan knew, but he needed him to say it, and hopefully realize how ridiculous it was.

"The crew thinks the bad luck is due to the girl."

"And what do you think, Fergus?"

"It does seem mighty suspicious that we're suddenly stuck in the Channel. We've never been stuck in the Channel before."

"And you think that slip of a girl controls the weather?"

"I could not say, Cap'n, but the crew is talking wild already and it hasn't been more than a few hours yet."

"And what is it they wish me to do, precisely?"

"Row her to the shore, sir."

The shore that was very likely twenty miles away.

Ronan cursed. "Can you not talk them down? The last thing I need is a mutinous crew. It's just the bloody Channel and as soon as this passes," he waved at the sky, "we will be on our way."

"Might I suggest something to pacify them?"

Ronan looked askance. "You mean give them extra grog so they will not care who or what happens to the ship?"

"Aye."

Ronan ran a frustrated hand over his face. "It could go awry. They could become more belligerent."

"They could," Fergus admitted.

"How about a compromise? They shut up and trust me and they will not be turned off when we make it to Ireland safely!" he barked.

Fergus puffed his cheeks, then blew out a breath.

"Shall I talk to them again? Truss them up like one of the horses and throw them in the brig?"

"I will speak to them." Fergus backed away warily.

Ronan had been in a sour mood before and now it was downright putrid, but it wasn't his crew's fault. Not entirely. "Give them an extra measure of grog for now," Ronan called after his second. "I don't want them cup-shot!"

"Aye, aye, Cap'n," Fergus called and continued hurrying away before Ronan changed his mind.

Unfortunately, the winds were no better when O'Brien and Kelly came to relieve his watch several hours later.

They approached him cautiously. They must have heard he was in the devil's own mood.

"Are the crew still mutinous?"

"Aye, Cap'n. They've been sitting idle all day. Idle hands are the devil's workshop."

"So instead of being grateful for being taken out of the miserable weather, they sit down there and stew about the girl."

O'Brien shrugged.

"Very well. Call for all hands on deck. They shall be idle no longer."

A shrill whistle followed this order, which subsequently produced a loud stomping and herding noise akin to stampeding cattle, though they only numbered near twenty. Soon, his crew was lined up, standing at attention as best they could through the pouring rain, looking at him like he was about to send them to their deaths in Davy Jones' locker.

"I will send them to their sleep too exhausted to think about any silly superstitions," he muttered before telling O'Brien to put them to work. "I want them swabbing the deck, pumping the bilges, working the rigging. Mending sails is too docile a job."

"Aye, aye, Cap'n." O'Brien turned and began ordering the men to their duties.

As for himself, Ronan climbed the rigging, not asking anything of his men he would not do himself. He needed to work so hard that he could think of nothing but the sheer pain of his muscles straining while he struggled to maintain his grip in the rain. He was just finishing a repair when the men stopped singing—if one were being generous enough to call vulgar sea shanties singing—and he looked down with a frown to see what was the matter.

He saw the looks of his men's faces before he saw the cause. His oldest crewman was scowling fiercely and Ronan followed his gaze. There stood Grace Whitford in her boy's breeches at the door of the companionway. She wore one of his oilskins draped about her shoulders and head, which did nothing to hide the wet clothing clinging to her long legs.

"*Oinseach*," he muttered to himself.

The members of his crew began crossing themselves and muttering Irish curses; some began to spit. Ronan swung down the rigging as fast as possible to put himself between them and the girl before they revolted and threw her overboard.

"Go inside now, ye daft lass! Lock the door, and do not come out again!" he yelled. The look on her face as it crumbled into fear and shame as she turned to flee his wrath shot an arrow straight through his heart. He cursed roundly, then turned towards his men. He was ready for a fight. "Who of you wants to be thrown in the brig for the rest of the journey?"

The look on his face must have frightened them, for they all turned back to their duties without another word.

Once they began moving again, he would make them apologize.

He should also post a guard at Grace's door, but there was no one he completely trusted at the moment beyond himself or Paddy, who would be no match for any of the men. With a heavy sigh, he knew he would also have to apologize later. But first, he needed more hard labour of his own.

CHAPTER 6

Grace ran back down the stairs, closed the door behind her and set the latch. She leaned up against it while she caught her breath. Her heart was pounding with fear. What had she done to anger Carew so?

They had spent the afternoon so pleasantly, and now it was as though a different person inhabited his body completely.

Shivering, she went over to the window seat and curled into a ball, the flannel wrapped tight around her as she watched the rain fall against the glass.

As if she hadn't been frightened enough, now her only ally seemed to be against her. She'd been brave and had not given in to tears again, but she was so very tempted, and her throat began to burn as she fought not to shed them.

Whenever she'd been upset before, one of her sisters had always been there to comfort her. That was clearly not an option, and she had no delusions that Carew would be willing to gather her in his arms and give her a kiss on the head, telling her everything would be well. The idea was laughable at best.

She gathered the sleeping Theo in her arms and held him against her chest. "You will have to do, my furry friend." He was rather good at comforting her once, but after a ferocious bout of self-pity, she decided escaping into another story was her best option.

Walking over to the bookshelf, she perused the titles again and stopped when she saw the one named *Persuasion*. It was by a lady author, Jane Austen, who had only recently been named after her death. Grace had read some of her other works that she'd now been named authoress of, and had not been surprised that a lady had written them. Grace would have been hard put to accredit the clever wit about young ladies' circumstances to a man. There had been entirely too much accuracy and understanding that she had yet to see in her brief experiences with the opposite sex. It was a shame the author had not been able to receive proper credit while she lived.

The beginning of the story did not capture her interest quite like Miss Austen's *Pride and Prejudice* had, with the best opening sentence Grace had yet to read in a novel. However, she persisted, and once there was mention of a sea captain, it immediately piqued her curiosity.

"I believe I know how the story will end, but what diversions will occur along the way until then?" Grace often liked to predict what the author might do, but the only thing she felt certain of was there ought to be a happy ending for Anne Elliot and Captain Wentworth. She was already inclined to dislike Sir Walter and Miss Elliot. They were most disagreeable, vain people—not to mention Lady Russell for her meddling—but it was the way of the world as they knew it, and Grace was fortunate she would be given the opportunity to choose. Yet there had already been two Seasons, and she had found no one to tempt her. That wasn't entirely true. Carew had tempted her from afar, but he had never noticed her. There had been no one else, she amended.

There was a knock on the door, and she reluctantly put down her story to answer it. She padded across the floor and lifted up the latch and looked out. It was Paddy, holding a tray.

"Food for you, miss." His brow furrowed as his gaze flicked downward, with an unmistakable curiosity in his eyes.

She held the door open for him to enter, then he set the tray on the table.

"I've brought your meal."

"Thank you, Paddy," Grace said warmly.

She couldn't miss the way his eyes lingered, his expression a mixture of confusion and bemusement as he set the tray down on the small table.

"Begging your pardon, miss," he said after a moment, straightening and scratching at his temple. "But I've never seen a lady wearing—" He gestured vaguely at her attire, his voice trailing off.

Grace glanced down at herself, suddenly aware of the loose-fitting breeches and oversized shirt that hung on her frame. She smiled, unable to help the laugh that escaped her lips. "Oh, these? I suppose it must look rather strange."

Paddy's eyes shifted nervously, but she didn't press him. He scooped up Theo and began to leave.

Paddy tilted his head, his curiosity evidently outweighing his hesitation. "Aye, strange is one way to put it, but I don't think I'd let the crew get a look at ye."

Too late for that, she mused. Is that what had angered Carew so? "Is it still raining?"

"Cats and dogs, miss. Do you need me to take Theo out?"

"Indeed, if you have a few moments to spare. I've been forbidden to leave the cabin."

Paddy's eyes shifted nervously, but she didn't press him. He scooped up Theo and began to leave the room, then stopped and turned around. "I almost forgot. Here's the string and feather that you asked for. I still need to bring the stick." He turned his pocket inside out and deposited the items on the table.

"What kind of knot will hold the string to this feather, Paddy?" Grace had sewn long enough that she was confident in her abilities, but thought the boy would enjoy being asked for his opinion.

As expected, he considered the two objects. "I've been learning my knots. All good sailors must know knots, you know. If you look at the ship closely, all of the sails and rigging have them," he said with amusing authority. "May I try?" he asked.

"I would be much obliged," she answered.

He handed the kitten to her, who immediately went for the bowl of food for himself. Paddy considered the two objects, then began to tie the string around the end of the feather. He must not have liked that one because he unravelled it and then started again. Grace did not interrupt him.

His tongue protruded as he performed his task, then he smiled hugely when he had finished. He held it up for inspection. "I used a reef knot."

"Well done," she commended, recognizing a simple square knot. "Once you find the stick, you may tie the other end of the string to it for me, and we will have a perfect toy for Theo."

He scooped the kitten up. "I'll bring him back in a bit, miss. I do not know why everyone is so afraid of you. You're not bad at all."

With that revelation, he left the room, leaving her dumbfounded. "Why are they afraid of me?"

She pondered the question at length, but would have no answers for several hours. Paddy had come and gone with Theo and after reading several chapters, Grace had taken a long nap.

When she woke, it was to a pair of deep blue eyes looking down at her softly. Blinking away the sleep, it took her a moment to remember that he had yelled at her but a few hours ago.

"Forgive me, lass. I did not mean to shout at you."

"Is it because the men are afraid of me?"

His eyes narrowed.

"Paddy let it slip."

"Aye. They are convinced the calm seas are because of bad luck."

"Bad luck?" she repeated in disbelief.

"There's an old belief that having a lady on board will anger the sea gods."

"Sea gods?" she whispered and pulled herself up on her elbows.

"They wanted me to row you back to England and 'twas why I called them up to do hard labour. They will be too tired now to worry about any superstitions. Just pray the winds begin blowing again by morning."

"At least they didn't demand I walk the plank."

"That a girl," he said gently, chucking her under the chin.

"You could row me back to England, you know. It would solve at least one of your problems."

"Have you any idea how long it takes to row twenty miles? Because we are at least that far from land." He began to pace across the cabin.

"Oh."

"And casting you away near World's End, England, would not solve any problems for me or you."

Grace supposed that was correct. At this point, she'd had plenty of time to think over what her journey alone and unchaperoned might be like days away from London. Facing rough men who thought she was a curse seemed like a better alternative. At least here she had Carew to protect her, and her family must know she was with him.

There was a knock on the door and Carew opened it to reveal Paddy again, trying to balance two trays one on top of the other. Carew took them from the boy, then placed them on the table.

They smelled delicious and Grace wondered if the food would taste as good.

She sat at the table as Paddy was dismissed, but noticed he took the kitten with him and smiled.

Earlier had been a stew with a distinctive ale flavour, but this was herring with roasted potatoes and leeks. She realized Carew was staring at her.

"Go on and eat, or my manners will escape me. I've worked up quite an appetite."

Grace obeyed. "This is delicious! I never expected such fine cuisine on a ship."

"We are fortunate that my cook is willing to come on short journeys. He'd never venture across the oceans. He grumbles nevertheless about having to limit his skills to such meagre tools. Secretly, I think he enjoys the challenge."

"Please send him my compliments. It is the best herring I've ever tasted."

"You should tell him yourself."

"I will when I am allowed out of the cabin," she retorted a bit sharply.

"Going to fling that hatchet at me every chance you get, eh?"

"Probably," she agreed. She'd never spoken to anyone like that save her sisters. What was it about this journey that was making her so bold? "Tell me about your home," she said, deciding a change of subject was in order. That afternoon's exchange was best forgotten. He seemed amenable to the switch.

"My family home," he corrected. "There's no beauty anywhere quite like Ireland."

Grace could hear the pride in his voice.

"Everything is greener than you can imagine. Our home sits atop a dramatic cliff, and when the skies are fair, you feel like you can see for eternity. The weather is very volatile there at times, but the views are worth it."

"That is something to look forward to, I suppose."

"Aye. You will like my sister, though she's a bit headstrong."

"Much like her brother?"

His lips quirked into a half-smile that she found ever so attractive. She'd fallen asleep every night of her first Season with that visage on her mind.

"No one is half so headstrong as me," he agreed.

"And your mother?"

"She's a dear. But she lives in daily fear of what will happen if Flynn has his way."

"Is he truly so bad?"

"Worse."

"Then please do not worry about me. Look to your family first."

"I'll not abandon you, Grace, but I must see to settling this."

Grace wondered if he truly despised her for this mistake, but was simply tolerating her until they reached Ireland.

~

Ronan cursed his resolve to stay away from his cabin, but he could not seem to stay away. If he need not apologize, he might have been able to see it through. Yet here he was, cursing his own weakness as he dined with Grace and, worse still, as his mouth formed another invitation he knew he would soon regret.

"It appears the rain has stopped. Would you care to stroll about the deck? Most of the men are down below at their own meal." He told himself it was a brotherly offer, something his sister might have enjoyed. That must be the reason for his stupidity, though it did little to settle his unease.

"If the rain has ceased, then I would love some fresh air."

He held out a hand to help raise her to her feet, then handed her the oilcloth she had used from before to wrap her in warmth. "It will be cool on the deck, though no breeze."

The smell of fresh rain mixed with brine was pleasant after being cooped up in the cabin. The deck was slick beneath their feet, the faint creaking of the ship the only sound to accompany the distant lap of water against the hull. Darkness enveloped them, save for the faint lantern glow. The damp night air sent a shiver through her, and he could feel her tremble even beneath the oilcloth. He led her to the bow, where the waters lay eerily still, disturbed only by the ship's gentle sway.

"Look up, lass," he commanded softly.

Her sharp intake of breath filled him with a quiet satisfaction that he was showing her something she'd never seen before. Her wonder mirrored his own every time he had the chance to marvel at the stars over an unbroken expanse of sea.

"Have you ever seen stars like this before?" He looked up and held his hands towards the sky.

She shook her head, her voice hushed with awe. "It is magical."

"There's nothing like the stars out on the water. They burn brightest when there's no moon."

He glanced towards the horizon, his thoughts briefly turning to the absence of moonlight. There being no moon worked against them moving more quickly, but he did not go into the tides and all of their idiosyncrasies. He was still hopeful the wind would at least be enough for them to start moving by morning.

"There are so many of them." She pointed towards the long streak of brightness. "It looks like a long, shining cloud with an explosion behind it, frozen in time."

"Greek mythology says that Zeus named it the Milky Way for the milk from his beloved Hera."

"It seems so much more magnificent than that name. Milk is too common."

"It was some thousands of years before. Perhaps there were not yet the words."

"True. And I am not certain I could come up with anything better myself. I am not sure there are words adequate to describe it now." Grace turned to look at him. "How are those tiny, twinkling stars suspended in the sky so far away, and we are still able to see them?" she asked, her voice tinged with childlike curiosity. Her innocent delight in one of his favourite things was intoxicating.

Ronan could not answer the question for which no one knew. "There are things even sailors and astronomers cannot explain," he admitted. "But that there are so many, and so constant, makes them our most reliable guides. Stars are the map we follow when all else fails."

She stared in silence for a long moment. "It's humbling, is it not? To think of how small we are—mere specks in the universe."

"Like a star," he murmured, though his voice carried a weight that hinted at a deeper meaning.

"Thank you," she said, so softly he barely caught it. "You could have left me in the cabin, but you did not. I do not know if I shall ever have the chance to see something like this again. I will treasure it."

Her gratitude both warmed and shamed him. 'Twas such a simple thing, and yet it had meant so much to her. "I count myself fortunate to be able to experience these things that many never will. Not everyone is able to understand the majesty—the infinity of what they are seeing. If I ever need to be humbled, the sea and sky are reminders of how powerless we truly are," he said after a moment. "The sea hasn't shown her full temper yet. It's hard to imagine her when she's angry."

"Perhaps I should try to speak with the sea goddess to pacify her," Grace suggested.

Ronan arched a brow but said nothing, letting the remark pass. Yet her next words struck a chord.

"I admit to your men terrifying me. It is as though they think I am a witch and wish to throw me in the water to see if I sink or float. Is there anything I can do to convince them otherwise?"

"Lass, nothing short of you commanding the winds to begin and having a smooth sail all the way home will convince them. 'Tis best to keep you away from them."

Her crestfallen expression caught him off guard. Clearly, she was unaccustomed to being disliked. It would be something for her to become accustomed to Irish ways and superstitions and sailors at that. He found himself softening his tone, despite the truth of his words. "The winds should shift soon. By morning, I believe we'll be moving again with the next tide."

"Are you only saying that for my benefit?"

"Mine as well."

A silence fell between them, broken only by the gentle lap of the water against the ship. For once, he allowed himself to bask in the rare peace of the moment, the sky above and her quiet presence beside him.

"How did you begin sailing?" she asked after a time.

Ronan pondered how to answer that. "I grew up on the bay. Water is a way of life for everyone there. Mostly fisherman," he replied, leaving out the darker ventures.

"But is not your passion horses?"

"Born of necessity," he said simply. Breeding horses had saved his family, a trade respectable enough to gain entry to England's elite. But it had required shipping, and so his life had become entwined with both land and sea. His men required talent for both horses and the sea, and he asked a lot of them. He asked a lot of himself.

The Irish peerage was not like the English. Yet running a business venture was not something one discussed amongst the *ton*. Horse breeding was one of those acceptable occupations gentlemen considered hobbies, and they were willing to pay obscene amounts of money for horseflesh.

Ronan leaned back slightly as he spoke. "After the potato famine, the estate needed more than rents to stay afloat. Breeding gave us something of quality to offer that couldn't be ignored."

His voice carried a note of pride as he continued. "We've sold to some of the finest stables in Ireland and England. The Earl of Denby is particularly fond of our hunters, and Lord Strathmore swears by the endurance of our carriage horses. They're special because we breed them for more than appearance. Strength, temperament, and intelligence—those are what make a horse truly great."

He met her gaze, his expression thoughtful. "Each horse that leaves Donnellan carries our name, our reputation; and it helps support more than just my family. The tenants, the workers—they all benefit from what we do."

"I wish it were possible for a lady to do such things."

"I do it because I must." A faint smile curved his lips. 'Tis not what the *ton* expects of a gentleman, but it's what keeps us standing."

"That is admirable. Why pretend otherwise?"

He looked at her, surprised by her boldness. Yet he knew she referred as much to his reputation. "'Tis not pretending, lass. I've simply no care to correct assumptions."

Her nod told him she perhaps did understand. Perhaps Grace was not so timid after all, but rather a woman who did not waste her breath on trivialities, rather didn't feel the need to trouble herself to compete for attention with those around her.

"So if you cede rights to this Flynn fellow, does that put your horse breeding in jeopardy?"

"Amongst other things. But I will never cede anything to the scoundrel."

A comfortable silence ensued as they both became lost in the wonder of the sky.

For a brief moment, Ronan pretended that there was nothing else in the world to worry about other than if the wind decided to blow. He could allow himself to enjoy the sounds of nature and peace around him. Perhaps even enjoy being in the presence of this woman. None of those things seemed meant to be for him—unless perhaps he could purge the earth of Donnagh Flynn. At the moment, the thought was fleeting and futile.

CHAPTER 7

Meanwhile, aboard *The Tempest*

"Why are we not moving?" Joy asked.

"I'm not sure. 'Tis deuced odd, but the wind has just stopped," Freddy remarked, seemingly as perplexed as she was. "Never seen that happen before."

They sat on one of the wooden chests that covered the deck. Mostly they held ropes.

"I hope it starts again. It will be difficult to reach Grace if we cannot move."

"I suppose they don't have wind either," he said reasonably as they stared up at the mast with the sails limp against it.

"This is rather tedious," Joy remarked. "It's not at all what I expected."

"It will get better if the wind picks up again. It is always windy in England."

Then Joy wondered what Patience and Ashley were doing—whatever the newly wedded did. They had not seen hide nor hair of them since they boarded, but to each their own. She'd much rather be on the deck, watching the world go by. If only it would start going by again.

"How do you think Carew reacted when he found Grace?" she asked.

"He was probably spitting fire."

"Like a dragon?" Joy asked.

Freddy seemed to ponder that. "They blow fire rather. Still, I cannot think he would be pleased. Now he will be shackled to her."

Grace might like that, but Joy wasn't sure. They had teased her about the Irish Earl, but Joy knew Grace the best and she wasn't certain that just because she found the man handsome that she would want to be married to him. They were very different. Joy was not sure someone like Carew could appreciate her quiet, bookish sister. Although she was only really quiet around strangers. Or if there were too many attention-seekers in the room. Then Grace didn't bother to compete. Joy admired that about her. For herself, Joy tended to draw attention, but not because she wanted it. That was why she had no desire to be part of Society. She drew the wrong kind of attention on accident.

"What do you think he will do to her? Lock her up in the brig?"

"Like a pirate? Aye, he might do something like that."

"Poor Grace. We have to start moving."

"I was not serious. He might lock her in a cabin, though."

"I realize that, but she must be very uncomfortable being unwanted on someone else's ship. The crew is all men."

"Not all men are dreadful." Freddy took offence.

"To be fair, I have never met another male like you. The sailors I met earlier were a bit rough."

"Carew will protect her even if he is displeased. Like a little sister," he reasoned.

"What is the worst that could happen to Grace?" Joy asked.

"He could refuse to marry her and ruin her."

"What a stupid, stupid thing ruination is. I truly hate that word," she huffed.

Freddy shrugged. "I do not make the rules."

"He would do that? Ruin her, I mean?"

"Westwood will not allow it," her best friend said with absurd certainty. Carew did not strike her as the type of person who would let anyone else dictate what he did or did not do. Rotham was a bit like that, too, except with a better reputation.

"Best keep it a secret that she's gone," Freddy remarked.

"That will never happen." Perhaps Joy spent too much time with the servants, but they knew everything that happened. "Unless Westwood bribes everyone, but with Rotham's servants and the Montfords', it's not possible."

Joy paced back and forth across the deck. "It should never have come to this," she muttered, her voice thick with guilt. "I am the one who left her on that ship. I didn't wake her, didn't make sure she disembarked with us. What kind of sister does that?"

Freddy looked up sharply. "Joy, you're being unfair to yourself," he said firmly. "It wasn't just you. There were several people who knew Grace had gone to rest. In the hustle and bustle of the wedding, no one remembered."

"That does not excuse it," Joy shot back, her eyes glistening with unshed tears. "I was the last person with her. I gave her Theodore to comfort her and left her there. She trusted me."

"You cannot take this all on yourself. It wasn't a deliberate neglect, Joy. It was an oversight—a mistake, yes—but not malicious. And it wasn't solely yours. Everyone was caught up in the wedding and the chaos of the day. And do you honestly think Grace blames you for this? If anything, she is probably blaming herself for not waking up."

Joy's shoulders slumped, the weight of her emotions pressing heavily on her. "I cannot bear the thought of her being hurt because of something I failed to do."

Freddy did not disagree with her. "That is why we are giving chase."

Hopefully, it would be enough.

A kitten poked its head from the pouch, and Freddy held up his finger for it to sniff before it scrambled out onto his hand. This one was an orange tabby like its mama, and Joy had named it Evelina. The little kitten climbed up his arm and onto his shoulder.

One thing Joy liked about Freddy Cunningham most was his smile and the pleasure he seemed to take in the little things. He was not overly complicated, but he was sunny and happy, and he loved animals as much as she. But most of all, he was comfortable and did not judge her as wanting because Joy knew she was not what was expected of a lady.

He laughed when Evelina settled down in the nook of his neck as though that was where she belonged.

"At least we have the kitten for entertainment," she said on a sigh as she reached for Evelina and scratched her chin.

"We are not very dashing rescuers, are we?" Freddy asked, though it warranted no answer.

Joy tended to be impulsive when impatient, and she very much liked the thought of being a dashing rescuer. What would one of her heroines do in a situation like this? "You are certain we cannot move without wind?" Joy asked Freddy.

"The boat is too large to row. The oars wouldn't reach the water," he explained very logically.

She huffed in frustration. "I do not like this at all."

While Joy was not happy about what had happened to Grace, she felt responsible for not remembering to make sure she was awake and had departed the ship. However, Joy was delighted to delay going to London, where it meant she would have to go out in Society. She would be quite pleased if that never ever happened.

As if things couldn't possibly get worse, a huge, fat raindrop landed on her head. She hated bonnets and took them off whenever she could get away with it. As it turned out, now was not a good time to be without one.

"I think it's raining," Freddy remarked as Joy was wiping water from her face.

He looked at the sky. "I suppose we should go to the cabin."

"I suppose we should," Joy agreed a bit sarcastically, though Freddy didn't appreciate or realize when she used it.

The ship was not as big as Carew's, and the Captain had relinquished his cabin to the newly wedded couple, which meant Joy had a tiny one to herself, and Freddy shared one with the Captain.

They squeezed into her tiny one because there was really nowhere else for them to go.

"Shall we play cards or read?" Freddy asked.

It was going to be a very long trip if they were stuck inside the small, smelly hole, Joy realized. Did they never clean? It smelled like a mixture of dirty sweat, urine, and sea-water.

They both had to sit on the berth because there was nowhere else to go. At that, Freddy had to hunch over because the ceiling was so low.

"I think a story. Did we bring any tales of pirates?"

"I do not think so but we can ask the Captain later. We do have *Robinson Crusoe*."

"That will do," Joy said as she leaned back and settled down to listen with the kitten curled in between them. Freddy did have a very soothing voice.

CHAPTER 8

Grace returned to the cabin sometime later, thinking she could not have devised a more perfect night. Were it in one of her stories, she might even have described it as romantic. To gaze at the stars on a mild evening, alone with the most handsome man she had ever beheld, seemed the ideal moment for him to place an arm about her shoulders and draw her close. Perhaps even to bestow a kiss upon her lips.

But alas, it was not a novel. She had felt gauche and insignificant beside him. Her sisters were often deemed Incomparables, and while she admired them, she had never felt their equal. Why had she even dared to imagine that a man like Carew—elegant and seasoned—would notice her? Most likely he thought of her in the same category as his younger sister. For one fleeting moment, Grace longed to be regarded as a woman, to possess the confidence her sisters exuded. They never doubted they were enough for their suitors. Instead, Grace hid behind them or a book, striving to blend in with the papered walls.

She fell asleep in her tiny cabin, having read by candlelight until the flame flickered out and left a faint trail of smoke.

Grace awoke to the sudden and unceremonious jolt of being

ONLY BY GRACE

thrown to the floor. The wind, which had been so serene, now howled with a vengeance. How could the weather shift so dramatically, from tranquil calm to a squall in an instant? She discovered a newfound respect for both Mother Nature and His Majesty's sailors, subjected to such capricious elements. As for the crew aboard this vessel, they could sink or swim for all she cared after the way they had treated her.

She sighed. She didn't truly mean it. Yet she had little doubt they might toss her overboard if Carew were not aboard. At least they were moving now; perhaps that would ease their hostility—one could hope.

The boat pitched and rolled, no longer gliding gracefully but bucking like a restless beast. A wave of nausea overtook Grace, enveloping her from head to toe. She thought ruefully of the expression 'green about the gills' and acknowledged its aptness. It was not a delicate shade of green, but rather something hideous and putrid. She struggled to her feet, only to collapse again, this time clutching a chamber pot. The ship's violent lurching mocked any attempt to retain her composure.

When her stomach had finally emptied itself, she lay curled upon the floor, weak and trembling. She yearned for fresh air, but there was no window, and the thought of venturing beyond her cabin filled her with dread. The acrid taste in her mouth was as vile as her ordeal.

At length, a knock sounded at the door.

"Come in," she croaked.

Paddy entered, lantern in hand, and recoiled visibly at the smell. "Cor, miss, you've been proper sick, ain't you?"

"Could I trouble you for some fresh water, Paddy?" she murmured, too drained to feel humiliated.

Covering his nose, the boy set the lantern down, took the foul chamber pot, and hurried out. Grace collapsed back onto the floor, relieved to leave the matter in his capable, if reluctant, hands.

When Paddy returned, he bore a clean pot and a steaming cup that smelled faintly of ginger. "Here's something for your stomach, miss," he said, offering the cup with a faint grimace.

Grace recoiled at the thought of ingesting anything but was touched by the boy's thoughtfulness. "Thank you," she whispered, taking the cup reluctantly. To her surprise, the ginger-honeyed brew soothed her raw throat. Her stomach convulsed, debating whether to accept or reject the intrusion. She stood quickly, determined to endure the discomfort at least until she reached Carew's cabin where she might find the solace of fresh air and a window.

With a trembling hand, she passed the cup to Paddy. "Hold this for me," she said, hurrying to Carew's cabin and closing the door behind her. She collapsed against the wall, gulping the fresh air like a lifeline. If this was a mere taste of life at sea, the next seven days promised to be a torment.

Even in Carew's cabin, Grace found little relief. Though the cabin afforded some fresher air, her rebellious stomach refused to be calmed by the ginger tea as the storm tossed the ship around like a toy in a child's hands. When Paddy returned to check how she did, he took the basin with a sigh.

"Please do not tell the Captain," she begged as another violent wave slammed the door shut and had them both holding on for dear life.

"I won't tell him on purpose," Paddy replied with the wisdom of someone far beyond his years.

"Is the crew at least pleased now that the wind is blowing?" she ventured.

Paddy shrugged. "I'm not sure they're ever really pleased, miss. But, aye, the storm will be your fault."

Grace groaned. "You might think my illness would soften their resentment."

"I doubt it," the boy said with a hint of pity. "You do have the worst case of the pukes I've ever seen."

"It is reassuring to be best at something," she muttered, while mulling over the word puke.

Paddy grinned faintly. "If there's naught else, miss, I've got to get back to work. All hands on deck, what with the storm."

As he turned to leave, a loud bang sounded against the door.

"What was that?" Grace whispered, hurrying to set the latch.

"Let me in, Paddy!" came a muffled shout. "I know you're in there!"

"Cor, it's Kilroy," Paddy muttered, his face pale.

"Who is that?" Grace asked, though she feared she already knew.

"The fiercest, meanest giant ye ever saw." Paddy trembled as the banging grew louder. Grace instinctively placed an arm around the boy. How sturdy was the latch? What did he want? She glanced around the cabin, searching for something to secure the door. Yet everything was bolted down, and there was nothing at hand with which to defend herself.

The voice outside grew more menacing. "Open this door, or I'll break it down and string ye up by yer toenails, boy!"

"Don't do it, Paddy," Grace urged.

Her gaze landed on a sword mounted upon the wall. Without a second thought, she seized it, though it felt impossibly heavy in her hands. As the door shuddered beneath another assault, Grace gritted her teeth and raised the blade. If they meant to harm her or Paddy, they would have to face her first.

The door rattled violently under Kilroy's assault, the splintering sound making Grace's stomach churn anew, though this time from fear rather than the storm's relentless tossing. The sword in her trembling hands felt impossibly heavy, its weight and her own terror conspiring to make her question her resolve. The blade quivered visibly, but she tightened her grip, willing herself to stand firm.

Paddy crouched beside her, his wide eyes fixed on the door. "Miss, I dunno how long that latch'll hold," he whispered, his voice barely audible above the furious pounding and the muffled roar of Kilroy's threats. "If he gets in—"

"He won't," Grace interrupted, her voice sharper than she intended. She glanced down at the boy, his youthful courage just barely holding against the tide of panic. "Stay behind me. No matter what happens."

Her mind raced. She wasn't made for this——this was the stuff of her sisters' daring exploits or the adventures in the novels she read.

Yet here she was, gripping a weapon meant for a soldier or brave fighter, neither of which she had remote claims to.

The storm outside seemed to echo his fury, a deafening crack of thunder rattled the timbers of the ship. Grace took a shaky breath, her pulse thundering in her ears. Her hands were clammy, and her legs trembled as the reality of this beast in front of her bore down on her senses.

"You're a coward, Kilroy!" she shouted with false bravado, surprising herself with the strength in her voice. "Only a brute would threaten a woman and child!"

A roar of laughter answered her from the other side of the door. The momentary silence that followed her words was deafening, broken only by the thrash of rain against the cabin walls and the creak of the ship.

Another crash sent splinters flying, and Grace felt the door begin to give way. She tightened her grip on the sword, lifting it higher despite the ache in her arms. If he came through that door, she would fight, though the very thought made her stomach lurch again.

The door burst open, slamming against the wall with a force that shook the cabin. Kilroy filled the doorway, his hulking frame as menacing as the storm that roared around them. His eyes, wild and bloodshot, fixed on her with deadly intent.

~

A STORM WASN'T MUCH BETTER than being becalmed, but they were moving now, at least. Ronan had been manning the helm after seeing Grace back to her cabin when the winds shifted and the first sounds of thunder rumbled in the distance. The sky, only moments before resplendent with celestial brilliance, now darkened to an ominous slate, streaked by bolts of jagged lightning that rent the skies with blinding majesty. Thunder intensified to a menacing growl that rattled the timbers. Then, as if impatient to enter the fight, the wind began to howl with unrestrained fury. Immediately, Ronan called for the entire crew to manage the sails and the rigging.

They had barely reached their posts when it began tearing through the sails with such force that they strained and shuddered under its unyielding onslaught. Waves rose like jagged mountains, then surged and crashed against the hull with a deafening roar, drenching the deck in torrents of painful knife-like brine.

The wheel, slick with rain, demanded all of Ronan's strength to hold its course, while the crew laboured with all their might to batten hatches and secure lines against the storm's relentless rage. The crew moved like shadows amidst the chaos, securing lines and shouting commands that were swiftly swallowed by the gale.

Ronan only had moments to think about Grace and hope she stayed in her cabin. He could only pray the crew was too occupied with manning the ship to blame the storm on their lady passenger.

His hopes were dashed before he scarcely had the thought. Never satisfied and always looking for reasons for the cause of every perfidy, Ronan saw the crew exchange furtive glances as they laboured upon the deck, then a few of them clustered together. Their voices and bodies, though subdued through the storm, carried a note of sullen dissent, betraying the simmering unease that had taken root since Grace's arrival.

He saw their expressions darken with mutinous resolve. As the ship's timbers groaned under the pressure of the waves, so too did their patience falter, threatening to splinter entirely.

The lanterns swung wildly, casting flickering shadows across the faces of the crew, whose expressions ranged from grim determination to abject fear. Amid this chaos, Kilroy, the giant with shoulders as broad as an ox, stood in the centre of the deck, a storm of his own brewing in his piercing eyes.

He strode forward, his boots pounding against the slick planks, until he stood nose-to-nose with Ronan. Despite the tumult around them, Kilroy's voice boomed like thunder, cutting through the clamour.

"Captain!" he roared, pointing an accusatory finger towards the cabins below. "Ye must do it! Toss the woman overboard, or we're all doomed to the deep! It's her, I tell ye. She's brought this devil's storm upon us!"

Ronan, standing tall despite the tempest, fixed Kilroy with an icy stare. His coat billowed in the wind, but he remained unyielding, gripping the railing to steady himself. "You dare to bring such madness to me in the midst of this gale?" he barked, his voice a whip of authority. "Get back to your duties, Kilroy, or you'll be the one I'll have to answer for!"

Kilroy's massive hand shot out, gripping the rail as though he meant to rip it from its moorings. "It's one person or all of us!" he bellowed. "We've seen it before, Cap'n. A Jonah aboard brings ruin to the crew! Ye may be too refined to admit it, but the men aren't fools. They see what I see."

"The only thing I see," Ronan said coldly, his voice cutting through the storm with a razor's edge, "is a coward seeking to blame his fear on a helpless woman. You shame yourself, Kilroy."

Kilroy's face darkened, his nostrils flaring. "Say what ye will, but we're on a cursed ship! The sea won't calm until she's gone. D'you mean to sacrifice us all for some lady? I'll not die for her!"

The men nearby hesitated in their tasks, glancing at one another and at Ronan, unsure whether to intervene. Ronan noticed this, his gaze flicking toward the wavering men.

"This ship will not be ruled by superstition," Ronan declared, his voice ringing with authority. "You'll do your duty, Kilroy, as will every man aboard, or I'll have you in irons before you can mutter another word of your nonsense."

Kilroy sneered, his teeth bared as the rain beat against his weathered face. "And how d'ye mean to enforce that, Cap'n, when half the crew agrees with me? Ye can't put us all in chains."

The tension crackled as fiercely as the lightning overhead. Ronan stepped closer, his voice lowering into a deadly calm. "Try me, Kilroy. But mark this—if you so much as lay a hand on her or incite another man to do so, you'll be answering to me personally. And I promise you, you'll wish the storm had taken you first."

For a moment, Kilroy stood frozen, his breath ragged, his massive frame taut with rage. But something in the Ronan's unyielding stare made him falter. With a curse, Kilroy spat onto the deck, turned on his heel, and stormed away into the chaos, barking orders to the men.

Ronan exhaled slowly, his grip on the railing tightening. The storm was far from over, and he knew Kilroy's rebellion had only begun. But for now, Grace below would remain safe—and as the captain, he intended to keep it so, no matter the cost.

Then came the cry—a piercing shout from above. All heads snapped skyward to witness Barry, the nimblest lad among them, slip from the rigging where he had been sent to adjust a stubborn sail. Arms flailed, legs kicked helplessly at the air, and for a heart-stopping moment, it seemed that the sea herself would claim him. Gasps of shock froze in every throat as he plummeted towards the deck.

A resounding thud brought all activity to a halt. Barry lay in a crumpled heap, groaning faintly but alive. The sailors surged forward, the crew's mutinous resolve momentarily forgotten as they surrounded their fallen comrade.

The collective breath of the sailors hung heavy in the air, their fear momentarily tempered by concern. Ronan pushed through the knot of men, cursing with a fluency that made even seasoned sailors blanch.

"Fetch O'Brien and Kelly!" he bellowed, his voice cutting through the howling wind and the crash of the waves against the hull. He gestured sharply towards the wheel, where his second-in-command wrestled with the helm. With an urgent nod, the man took over, bracing himself against the storm's wrath.

Meanwhile, as the men hovered to help Barry, their attention consumed by his injuries, Kilroy slunk away into the shadows, his towering form somehow blending with the chaos. His narrowed eyes gleamed with malicious intent as he slipped below deck, his movements swift and silent despite the storm's clamour.

Ronan wasted no time once being assured Barry lived. With a last glance at the boy being tended to, he turned on his heel and sprinted towards his cabin, each step precarious on the slick deck. His heart pounded, not from exertion, but from dread. He prayed he was not too late.

The door to the cabin exploded inward with a deafening crash, the splintering wood sending shrapnel scattering across the floor. Ronan's heart thundered in his chest as he raced towards the scene, knowing instinctively what he would find. The roar of the storm barely masked Kilroy's guttural snarl.

"Let me at the little witch!" Kilroy bellowed, his massive frame filling the doorway, his rage a palpable force. Ronan's pulse quickened as he caught sight of Grace. She was huddled with Paddy, pale and trembling, clutching each other behind the table as though it might shield them from the brute. The sight of her fear struck him like a blade to the chest.

Ronan pressed forward, his boots pounding against the deck, but the scene unfolded too quickly. Kilroy would see Grace cast overboard to appease his superstitions.

Grace's eyes darted to the sword in her hand, and Ronan could see her weighing her chances. Could she draw it in time? Even if she did, what hope did she have against Kilroy's brute strength?

Kilroy advanced, his heavy boots shaking the floorboards beneath his immense weight. "You've cursed us all," he spat, his voice venomous. He reached out a hand, rough and callused, towards Grace. "And I'll see to it that the sea takes ye before it takes one of my men!"

Grace screamed then, a sound that tore through Ronan's heart. She tried to heft the sword, her desperation evident in every movement. But before she could raise the blade, Ronan stormed into the cabin, his pistol already drawn.

"Enough!" he roared, his voice cutting through the chaos like a blade. His pistol was levelled squarely at Kilroy's chest, its gleaming barrel steady despite the violent rocking of the ship.

Kilroy froze mid-step, his hand mere inches from Grace's shoulder. His broad back stiffened, and he turned his head slowly to meet Ronan's gaze. The flickering lantern light revealed the sailor's drenched coat, his dark hair plastered to his brow, and a mask of fury carved into his features.

"Touch her, Kilroy," Ronan said, his voice cold and deadly, "and I'll send you to the depths myself."

The air in the room grew as taut as a bowstring. The storm's howl seemed distant compared to the silence that fell within the cabin. Grace's breaths came in shallow gasps, her wide eyes fixed on the pistol.

Kilroy's sneer faltered, uncertainty flickering in his narrowed eyes for the first time. He straightened slowly, his hand dropping to his side as though the weight of Ronan's words had struck him physically, his mutinous resolve wavering in the face of his captain's unyielding stance.

Ronan did not lower his pistol. His voice, when he spoke again, was laced with steel. "To the hull. Now."

Kilroy hesitated for a fraction of a moment longer before he stepped back. His rage clearly simmered still beneath the surface, yet he retreated without another word. Ronan remained in place, his pistol raised to follow.

"Are you harmed?" he asked Grace and Paddy with a quick sweep of his gaze over their persons.

They both shook with fright. "No."

"Go to the other cabin and lock the door. I'll return when I can."

CHAPTER 9

They moved to the dark, tiny cabin, but Grace was grateful for a door that would lock. Paddy followed her with Theo and a lantern and slid down to the floor since there was nowhere else to sit. The storm still raged on, the boat listing from side to side and front to back, causing Grace to hold on to the berth and try to think how she could possibly wake up from this nightmare and be in her soft, warm bed at Taywards instead.

"I wouldn't like to be Kilroy just now," Paddy said, wide-eyed and breathless.

"What do you think is happening?" Grace asked, but suspected she knew.

"The Captain is making mincemeat of him I'd wager. He'll get the cat-o'-nine-tails to be sure."

Grace sank on her knees to the floor. She did not know what that was, but it sounded horrid. "All because they think I'm cursed."

Paddy wisely did not comment.

At least she hadn't been sick again, she thought with twisted humour. Though every time the boat seemed to be lifted to the sky then drop, she expected the pukes—as Paddy referred to them—to return.

The sharp sound of hurried footsteps outside the cabin drew Grace's attention away from her thoughts. She had been trying to distract herself from what had just happened with Kilroy and the relentless swaying of the ship, but her nerves were still on edge.

"Unlock the door!" she heard Carew shout.

Paddy did as commanded. The cabin door swung open with a force that startled her, and there stood Carew, his face set in grim determination. Cradled in his arms was Barry, one of the younger sailors, his face pale and contorted with pain.

"Miss Grace, Paddy," Carew said, his voice steady but clipped. "I need your help."

Grace's breath caught as she took in the scene. Barry's arm hung at an unnatural angle, and though he tried to stifle his groans, they escaped through gritted teeth. The boy's skin was ghostly, damp with sweat, and smudged with grime. Blood stained the torn sleeve of his shirt.

Grace stood and came to his side without hesitation. "What happened?" she asked, her voice trembling.

"He fell from the rigging," Carew replied, carrying Barry through to his damaged cabin, then placing him on the table. His tone was brisk, but his movements were gentle as he eased the boy down. "His arm is broken, and he has cuts and bruises from the fall, but it could have been far worse. Paddy!" he barked, his voice carrying beyond the cabin.

"Aye, Captain?"

"Fetch clean water and cloths. Quickly," Carew ordered. Paddy nodded and darted off.

Grace moved instinctively, gathering the spare linens from the storage chest near the corner of the cabin. "Is there anything else I should do?" she asked, glancing nervously at the injured boy.

Carew looked at her, his blue eyes steady. "You'll need to help me splint his arm. Can you do that?"

She nodded, though her hands trembled slightly. "I can try."

Barry groaned as Carew began cutting away the shredded remains of his sleeve with a small knife. His arm was a mangled mess. The bone protruded through the skin, and the swelling was already severe. That caused bile to rise in her throat, and she pressed a hand to her mouth to stifle a gasp. She forced herself to look at the boy's face and steeled herself. The boy needed her, and this was no time for her weak stomach.

Paddy returned with a bucket of water and a stack of cloths, his face pale as he took in Barry's condition. "Here, miss," he said, handing them to Grace.

"Good," Carew said, taking one of the cloths and dipping it into the water. "Grace, hold his arm steady while I clean the wound."

Her heart pounded as she knelt beside Barry, gently gripping his arm as instructed. He flinched under her touch, his eyes screwed shut, and a whimper escaped his lips. "Be strong, Barry," she murmured softly. "The Captain will make it right."

Carew worked swiftly, cleaning the scrapes and assessing the break. His hands were sure and precise, yet there was a quiet compassion in his movements. "Paddy, find something sturdy for a splint—a length of wood, smooth and narrow," he instructed.

As Paddy scurried off again, Grace dabbed Barry's forehead with a damp cloth. His breathing was shallow, and tears leaked from the corners of his eyes despite his efforts not to cry. "You're being very brave," she told him, her voice calm despite her own inner turmoil. "We'll have you patched up soon."

Carew glanced at her, his expression softening for a brief moment. "Thank you," he mouthed quietly before returning his attention to the task at hand.

When Paddy returned with a piece of smooth timber, Carew set about splinting the arm with Grace's assistance. She held the boy as gently as she could, whispering soothing words as the Captain carefully aligned the limb and secured it in place with strips of linen. Barry cried out once, his voice raw with pain, but he did not resist.

Finally, the splint was in place, and Carew stepped back, wiping his hands on a cloth. "That should hold until we reach port," he said, his tone matter-of-fact but laced with relief. He looked at Grace and

Paddy. "Good work, both of you. Now fetch him a measure of grog to help him sleep, Paddy." The boy scurried off again.

Grace sat back on her heels, her hands trembling now that the task was done. She felt a wave of pride that she had managed to keep her composure, even as her heart ached for the injured boy. "Will he mend?" she asked softly.

"With rest, I hope," Carew replied. "Thank you."

She met his gaze, feeling a strange warmth at his praise. "I was glad to help," she murmured, though she knew it had been far more than she expected of herself.

After a measure of grog, Barry drifted into an uneasy sleep. Grace realized that the storm outside seemed less fierce, as though her own courage had somehow calmed the tempest.

Carew left to wash and put away the supplies he'd used, then attempted the repairs to the door latch that Kilroy had split open.

She sat quietly in the cabin, her gaze fixed on the boy now resting on the berth. Only moments ago, he had writhed in pain, his face contorted with agony as they worked to mend his broken arm. Now, to her relief, he had succumbed to the healing embrace of sleep. The rise and fall of his chest were steady, a small comfort amidst the chaos of this evening.

Her mind drifted to the rigging, impossibly high and treacherous even in calm weather. She had watched the sailors scurry up and down those ropes with an agility that seemed almost superhuman. That a boy should be sent aloft during a storm chilled her to the bone. How could such a task be required of someone so young, so vulnerable? The thought of Paddy up there, his small hands clutching the rigging as the wind howled and the rain lashed, sent a shiver down her spine. She knew enough of the world to understand that children often worked for a wage, but this—a life so fraught with danger—felt unbearable to contemplate.

And then there were the men. Her breath caught as her trembling began anew with all that had happened—how close to being thrown in the sea she'd been. These men truly believed her to be the cause of all their misfortunes, their anger and superstition so deeply ingrained that one of them had sought to end her life. Someone had wanted to murder her, and the realization was a blow that left her feeling fragile and exposed. But for Carew, she was certain she would have been cast into the sea, even now a feast for the sharks. It seemed unreal, yet hadn't women been burned at the stake for similar things?

She wrapped her arms around herself, her fingers gripping the fabric of her clothing. The memory of Kilroy's rage, the violent pounding on the door, and the moment the latch had begun to give—all of it replayed in her mind, each scene more horrifying than the last. How had it come to this? She had never imagined her quiet, unassuming life would lead her to the brink of hell.

The creak of the cabin door made her start, and she looked up to see Carew enter, holding tools. "The latch is repaired, you may rest there safely tonight. I'll stand watch."

There was a calmness about him, as though the events of the storm and the confrontation with Kilroy had left no mark upon him. He glanced briefly at the sleeping boy, his mouth curving into the faintest smile. "The grog works every time," he murmured, more to himself than to her.

"Why on earth would such a small boy be sent up the rigging in the midst of a violent storm?" she demanded, her indignation again overcoming her caution. "Surely, putting a child in such danger defies reason?"

Ronan met her gaze steadily, his expression tinged with both understanding and the weariness of experience. "I understand your concern, Grace," he said evenly. "But the boys aboard a ship, even one as young as Barry, know the risks. They are raised to understand the sea's dangers and the part they must play to keep us all alive."

"But a child," she pressed, her voice softening with incredulity. "Surely his life is worth more than the speed of climbing a mast."

"Aye," Ronan said, his tone steady but firm. "And it's that very speed that can save lives. Barry's size and agility make him better suited for tasks that even the strongest man might fail at in time. A delay in securing the sails could mean losing the ship—or worse."

Grace hesitated, her concern shifting. "And now? What will become of him?"

Ronan sighed, his voice also softening. "Barry's spirit won't let him be idle for long. But I'll see to it he takes on lighter tasks until he's properly healed. It's his world, Grace. The sea shapes us all—young or old."

Grace studied him, marvelling at how he could behave so normally after such an ordeal. He had fought both the storm and a murderous giant with a composure she could scarcely fathom. And now here he was, as though it were any other day.

But when he turned and caught her gaze, his expression changed. His sharp eyes softened, and in that moment, he seemed to see everything: her fear, her inadequacy, her lingering thoughts of the men who had wanted her dead. She looked away, unable to meet his piercing gaze.

Evidently recognizing the state she was in, he set down the tools with a purposeful clatter, his movements brisk and efficient. "Grace," he said gently, his voice low but firm. He crossed the small space between them, gathering her up in his arms. "You're safe now."

The warmth of his touch steadied her, but her throat burned with tears. "He wanted to kill me," she whispered, the words tumbling out before she could stop them.

"I know, but he did not," he replied, his tone resolute.

"But if you had not been here—"

"I was here," he interrupted, crouching slightly to meet her eyes. "I shall not let anyone near you again."

His reassurance should have soothed her completely, but it only made her wonder what might happen next. What if the men turned on him for protecting her? What if the storm worsened? What if—?

"Stop tormenting yourself," he said, as though he could read her thoughts. "It is over."

Confused by her feelings, she dared to look up into his face, to see if he might be feeling what she did not understand. His eyes were dark and intense, but he said nothing. Their breaths intertwined, and before she knew what was happening his soft lips were upon hers as though the butterfly had chosen its place. It was over with quickly—almost chaste but for the feelings it stirred inside her.

Not wanting the moment to end, she lowered her head against his chest. They stood like that for some time, as though he was also receiving some solace from her. He gently kissed the top of her head and whispered in Gaelic to her things she did not understand, but warmed her nonetheless.

For the first time that night, Grace allowed herself to relish the comfort of his presence. Grace felt, perhaps foolishly, that as long as he stood with her, everything would be well.

∽

THE STORM, which had raged with fury, at last gave way to a blessed steady wind. The skies cleared, revealing a vast expanse of azure above, and the sea, though restless, rolled with a gentler rhythm. *The Selkie* surged forward, her sails filled with the brisk wind, as though eager to make up for time lost in the tempest. The mood aboard lightened with the weather, and Ronan knew if he brought Kilroy on deck for punishment, it could shatter the thin layer of peace they had settled into.

It was best to deal with him later, though normally he knew it was preferable to deal with discipline immediately. Punishment was the worst part of captaining a ship, he thought grimly, and would very likely shatter his own thin mask of being a gentleman. Thankfully, he did not have to captain a ship full-time. He did not know if his constitution could bear it.

Ronan had scarcely slept, the image of Grace's pale face etched in his mind, her wide eyes betraying a fear she had been too brave to voice. That wretched Kilroy—his arrogance, his cruelty—it was a miracle Ronan had restrained himself from killing him. The impulse to strike the cur down, to make him pay for so much as looking at Grace with disdain, had burned hot in his chest. It was a fury unlike anything he had known, so raw and primal that it startled him. For a gentleman to lose control was unthinkable, and yet, in that moment, the thought of protecting Grace outweighed all else. And therein lay the rub. What was he to do with these feelings?

The question of what to do about Grace was far from simple. It was not merely a sense of duty or honour—no, that he could have accounted for, managed with reason and restraint. But this...this was something more, a protectiveness so fierce it bordered on possessive. The idea of her being hurt, frightened, or even spoken to without care was intolerable. It was similar to the rage he felt towards Flynn on Maeve's behalf, was it not?

He'd almost lost control and fully kissed her last night. The feel of her trembling in his arms had been almost too much to withstand.

'Twould be for the best to protect her from a distance, with the polite indifference of an acquaintance. He could keep her safe from his crew and pray the weather held and the journey was swift. Four more days, if the sea goddess was kind. He scoffed mockingly.

All this, and he needed to turn his attentions to dealing with Flynn.

Ronan paced the length of his mate's cabin, his thoughts as restless as his pacing. His hands clenched and unclenched at his sides, betraying an agitation he would never display before his crew. Flynn. The very name curdled his blood. That base, double-dealing scoundrel, whose every word dripped with false charm, now loomed like a storm cloud over all that Ronan held dear.

It was Maeve he thought of most—Maeve, his sister, whose bright spirit and generous heart had been both her greatest virtues and her gravest vulnerabilities. From the moment Flynn had manoeuvred an introduction to Maeve, Ronan should have perceived his intent. Flynn was no suitor besotted by Maeve's wit or grace. He was a predator, circling his prey with cunning eyes, intent upon capturing her to exact revenge. And now, with Ronan away in England, the trap was sprung.

Ronan's jaw tightened, his stride growing more forceful as he rehashed in his mind all he knew of the situation. Flynn had woven his web with care, insinuating himself into Maeve's innocence, whispering falsehoods, until she had begun to trust him. Trust! The very notion was a bitter irony, for there was no man alive less worthy of it.

He paused at his berth and bowed his head. Could he have acted sooner? Should he have seen more clearly, intervened more decisively? The answers mattered little now; the time for regret was past. Action—swift and resolute—was all that remained.

Flynn had manipulated Maeve like a carefully crafted chess game, with Ronan the king he really longed to capture. He felt his stomach twist at the thought of Maeve bound to such a man—a lifetime's torment for the price of a single moment's carelessness and naïveté. No, he could not, would not, allow it.

And yet, Flynn was not a foe to be lightly dismissed. He was undeniably clever, and possessed of a ruthless nature. He would play this game with skill, anticipating each move, countering each defence. Carew could see the man's smirk even now, as vividly as if he stood before him. Flynn would be waiting, confident that Ronan would arrive too late or act too rashly, leaving Maeve unprotected.

But Flynn had miscalculated. For whatever else the world might say of Lord Carew—none could accuse him of abandoning his duty—and Maeve was his duty. More than that, she was his family, his blood, the bright spot in a life too often shadowed by obligation and restraint. To fail her now would be to fail himself utterly.

Ronan straightened, his resolve hardening like steel tempered by fire. The same determination that drove his ship through the storm and tempest now propelled him forward. Flynn might think himself the master of this game, but he had not reckoned on Ronan's will. Not with his sister at stake.

Flynn thrived on deception and manipulation; his success built on the ignorance of his adversaries. Ronan would deny him that advantage and dismantle Flynn's schemes. There was no doubt in his mind that Flynn would be dishonourable. He knew Ronan would never agree to a holy union with Maeve, nor concede power.

And then there was Maeve herself. Ronan's heart ached as he thought of her, alone and perhaps frightened, caught in a snare she had not even seen until it was too late. He had always strived to protect her, but had he done so at the cost of her independence? Had his watchfulness left her ill-prepared to recognize a villain like Flynn?

These were questions he could not yet answer, but he vowed to make amends. Maeve's spirit was too strong to be broken, too bright to be dimmed by a man like Flynn. Ronan would see to it that she regained her confidence and her freedom.

Turning from the berth, Ronan moved to the small window and gazed out at the restless sea. The horizon lay shrouded in mist, a veil of uncertainty over the days to come, but beyond it lay Ireland and with it the chance to set things right. He would see his sister safe, no matter the cost. Flynn might be clever, but Ronan's determination was boundless, and when it came to Maeve, there was no force on earth that could stand in his way.

His thoughts turned back to the present, to Grace. He could not ignore her for the remaining days because he was a coward. He was unsure how he felt after he'd held her the night before. In the light of day, it could all have been some otherworldly experience between the storm, Kilroy, Barry, and the kiss.

It was becoming more difficult not to see Grace in the light of a desirable female. Who was he kidding? She certainly was that, but was he thinking differently because she would, most likely, be his wife? He still thought it best for her to find a more worthy man if she still had the choice.

Yet he could not seem to stop himself from thinking about her. It was difficult not to make excuses to visit the cabin. To want to dine with her—to check how Barry went on because he knew she'd be there.

It was, in fact, close to the midday meal—he could tell by the smell of roast pork coming up from the kitchen. As he walked in that direction, he decided it would be doing Paddy a favour since he had extra duties, so he went to fetch their trays, like the apparently besotted fool that he was.

It was no small feat to knock on the door holding two trays, but he decided to use his boot. Grace had been instructed to keep the door locked at all times, and he knew she would not need reminders as to why.

"It is I, lass."

When he saw her smile, it both warmed his heart and terrified him. She looked at him with such tenderness and warmth and he knew he had best be careful or she would no longer have a choice in whom she married. He felt compelled to warn her, but they still had a few days until they reached Ireland and he told himself he'd behave in the way he would to Maeve.

"What has Cook prepared today?"

"Roast pork, if I'm not mistaken."

Ronan stepped inside the cabin, balancing the trays carefully before setting them down on the small table. Grace had already begun clearing a space, her movements graceful and efficient. He watched her for a moment, taking in the way her hair caught the light filtering through the cabin window and the way her lips curved slightly as she worked. She turned to him, catching his gaze, and raised a brow.

"Do I have smudge on my face, or are you merely pondering some great naval strategy?"

"Neither," he replied smoothly, though he felt a smile tug at his lips. "I was merely admiring your remarkable ability to make even the simplest of tasks appear graceful."

Grace laughed softly, the sound warm and infectious. "Is this the flattery for which you earned your sobriquet?"

"Who said anything about flattery?" he countered, his voice dropping slightly. "I'm merely stating facts, Miss Whitford. Would you rather I resort to naval strategy for conversational inspiration?"

She gave him a mock serious look as she began to lay out their meal. "I suppose that would depend. Would it involve roast pork?"

"Not unless the Admiralty has developed an appetite for Cook's fine culinary skills," Ronan replied, stepping forward to help. His fingers brushed against hers as he passed her a plate, and for a fleeting moment, the cabin seemed to grow warmer.

Grace met his gaze, but she did not look away. "It would seem that you are determined to be charming today."

"Charming?" he echoed, his brow lifting. "Now that, I assure you, is not deliberate. I save my charm for disarming mutinous crews."

"Then I shall consider myself honoured to be subjected to your unintentional efforts."

"Woe be to you when I use it on purpose."

Ronan glanced at Grace, noting the shift in her expression. Her brow furrowed and her lips pressed together as though weighing her next words. He braced himself, sensing the direction of her thoughts even before she spoke.

"What of Kilroy?" Her question was careful but insistent. "What will become of him after what he did?"

Ronan's jaw tightened at the mention of the man's name. He looked away out of the window where darkness was falling. "He's in chains," he said at last, his voice even. "Confined below deck where he can do no more harm."

Grace nodded, though her expression betrayed no satisfaction. "And once we dock?"

Ronan met her gaze. "He will be dismissed from my service permanently. Men like Kilroy have no place aboard my ship, nor in my trust."

"But will that be enough?" she pressed, her tone tinged with unease. "He might find his way onto another crew, where he could harm others, or back to you for revenge."

Ronan sighed in frustration. "It is possible. But I can see to it he's no longer a danger to my men. Beyond that, justice will find him soon enough."

She studied him for a moment, then nodded, her faith in him evident despite her lingering concerns. "I trust you will do what is right."

He hoped her faith in him was not misplaced.

CHAPTER 10

The days passed with a strange sense of suspension for Grace, each one merging with the next as the ship cut steadily through the waves under fair winds. The crew seemed to have swallowed their spleen, and had settled into their work with solemnity. It appeared they had decided to tolerate her presence—or, at the very least, ignore it. She dared not venture near them, preferring instead to keep to the cabin that Lord Carew had graciously surrendered for her use, even though it seemed as though he himself avoided her. She could hardly blame him. How he must be ready to be rid of her!

Within the close quarters, she busied herself as best she could, though the hours stretched long and tedious. She had retrieved *Persuasion*, and Grace now found herself grateful that Miss Austen had spared her readers the details of life at sea. The reality was less romantic than her imagination had envisioned when first hearing of Captain Wentworth's occupation.

The book offered some solace from her restless thoughts, though she read only in fits and starts. Her mind often wandered, straying to the events that had brought her aboard and to the uncertain future awaiting her. She tried to concentrate on Anne Elliot's struggles, drawing some comfort from the heroine's quiet strength, but it was difficult to immerse herself fully when the sound of creaking timbers and the rocking motion of the sea reminded her constantly of her surroundings.

At least she was not entirely alone. Paddy had less time since he was helping with the injured Barry's chores. Barry was convalescing in her cabin, and Grace made it her duty to check often how he did. Though her knowledge of medicine was limited to household remedies, she brought him simple comforts—playing cards or reading him snippets of books to distract him. Barry had taken a liking to Theodore, and he delighted in coaxing the kitten into chasing the feather on a string Paddy had fashioned.

If Barry had not been there to keep her company, she might very well have gone mad thinking of how she had made of mess of everything, even if unwittingly. It had been three long days since the storm and all that had happened with it. Three long days in which her imagination had gone quite wild. It had begun its love affair with Carew again. However, this time it was out of respect for his depth of character—his calm strength and command—his duty to his family. Her sense of unworthiness grew. What had she ever done to earn such an epithet? The most worthy thing she had ever done was knit mittens for the poor.

As if she'd conjured him merely by thought, Lord Carew knocked at the door. She opened it to see his imposing frame filling the narrow doorway. He regarded her with a measured expression that Grace had come to recognize as his version of concern.

"Good afternoon," he said with a slight bow. "I have just come from seeing Barry."

"He is doing well," she remarked as she set her book aside, grateful to have sight of him again, even though her nerves tingled at his presence.

"I'm allowing him to perform some light duties again. He tells me he is about to climb the walls. Have you ever heard of such a notion? I suppose when you are used to climbing rigging, why not walls?"

Grace laughed. "I am afraid that is true, but also a good sign that he is healing."

"I must thank you for caring for him. It eased my mind to know he was being looked after while I dealt with other things."

Grace would not ask what those other things were.

"Barry's plight made me think that perhaps you, too, might be desiring a change of scene. Would you like to venture on deck?"

Grace hesitated, a dozen objections rising to her lips. The prospect of facing the crew, even with Lord Carew at her side, was daunting. "Are you certain it is safe?" she asked, her voice betraying her uncertainty.

His brow arched slightly, a trace of amusement softening his chiselled features. "Safe enough, provided you give the men a wide berth. They have their work, and you need not concern yourself with their opinions. Come, you will find the sky far more pleasing than these walls."

Carew offered his arm as though they were promenading through a London park rather than the deck of a ship and as though someone had not tried to kill her a few days before. She stood and smoothed down her dress, not bothering to fetch her bonnet or gloves.

The change of scenery was startling after days below. The deck stretched wide before her, a sharp contrast to the last time she'd been above which had been at night. The vastness of the sea spread out in every direction, its blue expanse dazzling under the sunlight. The breeze was brisk but not unpleasant, carrying with it the tang of salt and the freshness of open air. Grace inhaled deeply, feeling a tension she had not realized she carried begin to dissipate.

Carew led her to a quiet corner of the deck, away from the more active areas where the crew was notably absent. He gestured towards the railing, and she stepped cautiously forward, peering over the edge. The sight of the bow cutting through the waves, cresting and falling endlessly, was mesmerizing.

"You see," he said, his tone almost conversational, "there is little to fear here now. The sea can be a harsh mistress, but on a day like this, the punishments are worth the rewards."

Grace turned to him, surprised by the poetic quality of his words. There was a depth to his voice, an undercurrent of reverence for the ocean that she had not expected. "It is beautiful," she admitted, though she could not entirely banish her unease. "But it was less the sea than the people I was afraid of. I do not suppose I will receive credit for the favourable weather."

Carew regarded her with an amused expression. "I would not count on it. Shall we remind them of your powers?" He raised a brow as a challenge. "They may yet regard you as a talisman."

"Of course." Her tone indicated she would do nothing of the sort.

He chuckled. "You presume to apply logic to the situation, of which very little is to be had with superstitions."

"I am pleased enough to be ignored."

"A lady such as yourself is unlikely to pass unnoticed for long, even amongst the most superstitious of sailors."

Grace tilted her head, her own amusement flickering in her expression. "You mistake me for my sisters. I am noticed by association."

"Nay, lass. I am not mistaken."

He looked at her meaningfully, but she dared not hope nor argue, for it was pointless. She knew the truth. While she was no antidote, her sisters were all stunning—not just for their beauty, but for their inner light that shone like the stars she and Lord Carew had witnessed the other night. He was simply being kind.

"You have borne your situation with more composure than most would muster."

His words warmed her, though she was uncertain whether to believe them. "I fear I have done little to earn such praise, my lord. I have merely endured what I cannot change."

"Sometimes," he said quietly, "endurance is the greatest test of all."

They stood in silence for a time, the wind whipping at her hair and face, and the sound of the waves filling the space between them. Grace found herself oddly at peace, the vastness of the sea lending perspective to her worries. Whatever lay ahead, she would face it with as much resolve as she could summon. For now, she allowed herself to enjoy the rare moment of tranquillity, standing beside a man who seemed to understand her plight better than she could have imagined.

Their gazes met, and for a moment, the playful words fell away, replaced by a quiet understanding that neither could quite articulate. A gust of wind caught her by surprise, and Grace looked away to grasp the railing, her heart inexplicably lighter, even as her thoughts grew more tangled than ever. Maybe he did see a little light within her that others had missed, and a twinkle of hope began to flicker in her breast.

~

Ronan stared thoughtfully at Grace as she spoke, her words tumbling out in a way that suggested she was entirely unaware of the effect she had on those around her. Did she not know that her beauty would halt legions of soldiers on the march to war? She would always draw eyes, even as she aged, he suspected. He'd noticed her beauty from the start. It had been her timidity that had made him dismiss her.

He had known many women who were conscious of their charms, who wielded their beauty like a weapon. But Grace was different. There was a naturalness to her, a lack of artifice that made her all the more captivating, now that she'd opened up. Even he had been slow to see it at first. She seemed wholly unaware of the way her eyes sparkled when she laughed, or how the faint flush that coloured her cheeks in moments of emotion only heightened her appeal. She carried herself with a modesty that was neither feigned nor excessive, and yet there was an underlying confidence to her that fascinated him. It was a paradox—a delicate balance of meekness and strength that he could not quite unravel.

And therein lay the mystery. Was it her very blindness to her own beauty that made her so intriguing? Or was her modesty born of something else entirely—perhaps a life spent overlooked by those closest to her, or undervalued in the shadow of more lively siblings? The thought unsettled him, for he could not bear the idea of such a light going unrecognized, of Grace doubting her worth simply because she had not been taught to see it herself.

A curious resolve began to take root in Ronan's mind. He wanted her to see herself as he saw her: not merely as a young lady with pleasing features, but as a woman of quiet brilliance and enduring charm. He wanted her to understand the power she held, not to wield it over others, but to carry it with pride.

It was an unfamiliar desire, one that unsettled him even as it took root. For what business had he, a man bound by duty and circumstance, to concern himself with a young maiden? And yet, he could not seem to help himself. Grace had a way of drawing him in, her unassuming presence casting a subtle spell on him. If he could accomplish nothing else during this unexpected voyage, he would at least endeavour to plant a seed of self-awareness in her heart—a recognition of her own worth that no storm or scandal could ever erase.

It was nothing he had undertaken before, and yet he found himself wholly committed to it. She had become his responsibility, for better or worse. To protect her from ruin if necessary. If Grace could see herself as he did, then she would have the strength to face anything. And Ronan wanted that strength for her more than he cared to admit. 'Twas something small he could do for her even if he was bound to fail her in every other way. If only they could weather this trial with her reputation intact, she could still find herself a worthy husband. That thought pained him even though he knew it was for the best. If he was being honest with himself, it was not pain in the same way it was with Maeve.

"How many more days, do you think?" Grace asked, interrupting his dangerous ponderings.

Ronan glanced at the sails, the taut lines, and the steady motion of the ship before answering. "If the winds continue at this pace, I expect we'll arrive by morning." He was both relieved and dreading it at the same time.

"So soon? I confess, I shall be glad to set foot on land again." Her face lit with relief, which ironically made him wish she'd enjoyed the journey more—that his crew hadn't begun to strip away her innocence and show her the cruel world.

A gust of wind carried her scent to him—something floral but piquant, and unexpectedly intoxicating. Ronan found himself momentarily unmoored, the scent conjuring more thoughts he had no business entertaining. He turned his gaze back to the sea, seeking refuge in its vastness.

The impending arrival of what awaited him in Ireland weighed heavily on him. Every mile they crossed brought them closer to the confrontation he dreaded yet knew was inevitable. Flynn. Even the thought of the man's name set his jaw on edge. And Maeve—his sister, bright and trusting—caught in a web of deception he could not yet untangle.

"Do you wish to talk about it?" Grace's voice penetrated through his dark thoughts.

"Nay, lass. Talking will not make the problem go away. I'm anxious to have it over and done."

She nodded her understanding and he watched as her face became distracted, then transform.

Ronan followed her gaze as she leaned forward with unabashed enthusiasm. Then he saw the cause: a pod of humpback whales, their sleek, dark bodies cutting through the waves with graceful precision. One leaped skyward, its massive form momentarily airborne before crashing back into the sea in a cascade of foam. Another followed, its tail slapping the water with a sound and splash that echoed across the ship. The pod seemed to revel in their performance, as though they were aware of their audience.

But it was not the whales that held Ronan's attention. No, it was Grace. Her entire being seemed alight with wonder, her face glowing with an innocence and unfiltered joy that left him entirely disarmed. She turned to him suddenly, her eyes wide and sparkling.

"Have you ever seen anything so magnificent?" she exclaimed, her voice trembling with awe. "Look at them! They seem so free, so alive. I did not think anything could equal seeing the stars."

"I have seen whales before, yes," he admitted, his tone far softer than he intended, "but I cannot say I have ever looked at them in quite the way you do."

Her brow furrowed slightly, though the corners of her mouth remained lifted in a smile. "And how is that, my lord?"

He hesitated, his words catching somewhere between his mind and his tongue. How could he explain that her reaction, so unguarded and genuine, had struck him more deeply than the sight of the whales themselves?

"You see them as though they are a gift," he said at last, his voice quieter still. "As though they exist purely to delight."

"And do they not?" she asked, her head tilting with a mix of curiosity and challenge. "Surely such a spectacle must be meant to remind us of the beauty in the world, of the joy that can still be found, even in unexpected places. That there is a whole world beneath the surface of the seeming infinity of the ocean."

Her words hung in the air between them, simple yet profound, and Ronan found himself momentarily lost for a reply. She turned back to the whales, her fingers gripping the railing as though anchoring herself to the moment, her laughter spilling out once more as another whale breached the surface then sprayed a fountain from its spout.

Ronan watched her, his chest tightening with something he could not quite name. There was a purity to her joy, a refusal to be diminished by their circumstances, that both moved and unsettled him. He had spent so much of his life guarding himself, locking his heart away behind walls of duty and a roguish exterior. Yet here she was, this woman who had been thrust into his world without warning, peeling back those walls with nothing more than her laughter, her wonder, her presence.

The thought shook him, and he turned his gaze back to the sea, his expression momentarily grim. He could not allow himself to feel this way, not now. His path was already set, his responsibilities too great to indulge in something so…fleeting. And yet, when he glanced back at her, all his resolve seemed to falter. What would she think if she knew?

For a moment, the air between them seemed to shift, the space narrowing despite the openness of the deck. Grace looked away, back towards nature's display, her lashes lowering as though to shield herself from whatever she might see in his eyes. Ronan felt the urge to step closer, to bridge the gap entirely, but he held himself back. What was he doing? This was neither the time nor the place for such thoughts, and yet they persisted, unwelcome and undeniable.

Grace turned to him again, her cheeks flushed, her breath quickened with excitement. "You should smile, my lord," she said, her voice teasing but not unkind.

Ronan blinked, taken aback by her boldness, but before he could reply, she turned back to the whales, her attention entirely on their joyous display. He allowed himself the smallest smile then, a quiet indulgence he could not quite suppress. To be as pure as her. If only he didn't feel the weight of the world on his shoulders, he could indulge in it.

And as he stood there, watching her light up at the sight of the whales leaping once more into the morning sun, he felt an unfamiliar warmth stir within him. It was a dangerous feeling, he knew—this enchantment she seemed to weave so effortlessly—but in that moment, he did not have the strength to resist it.

It was being on the ship that made life shrink to a microcosm that made you forget what else awaited you in the vast world. Like Donnagh Flynn.

Morning could not come soon enough. And yet, as he stood there beside her, the prospect of parting from Grace filled him with a strange and unfamiliar ache. It was a feeling he could not name, and he was not entirely certain he wanted to.

CHAPTER 11

*G*race was afraid she had not been completely honest, she reflected as she lay in her berth for the last night, her fingers absently stroking Theo as he purred. The ship rocked gently beneath her, a soothing motion she had come to associate with comfort rather than discomfort. If she could take away the man who had tried to kill her, then she would have described the voyage as the most wonderful time of her life. Also perhaps, she amended, save the seasickness, but since that only seemed to be when the weather was exceptionally severe, she could overlook that part. That seemed a minor nuisance compared to the extraordinary moments that had filled the days in between.

While she was looking forward to Ireland, she was not looking forward to being parted from Carew. She'd had his full attention at times on this journey, and it had been beyond her childish dreams. His attention, even though received by accident, had become something she cherished more than she ought. For once she had felt seen by him instead of found wanting.

And yet, there was an unpredictability to him that left her uncertain in more ways than one. One moment he was warm and engaging, his sharp wit and keen intelligence transforming their conversations into a lively dance that left her mind alight and her heart racing. But then he would retreat into himself, becoming distant and inscrutable. Had she imagined the connection between them entirely? What version of Carew awaited her once they reached Ireland? Would he withdraw from her completely, an obligation now fulfilled? The thought gnawed at her, though she tried valiantly to push it aside.

The problem with fairy tales was that reality eventually intruded. Take *Persuasion*, for example. While Anne Elliot's steadfast patience had earned her a triumphant reunion with her Captain Wentworth, Grace could not bring herself to expect the same happy ending for her own tale. Lord Carew was nothing at all like she'd first thought him. It was possible, she supposed, that his particular manner aboard the ship —his attentiveness, his occasional warmth—was an anomaly, a reflection of the confined setting rather than his true character. It was also possible she was getting a rare view of the real man...unguarded and unfiltered. That possibility more than any other unsettled her, for she wanted to keep him.

A sharp knock at her cabin door startled her from her sleep. Rising quickly, she smoothed her impossibly wrinkled skirts and opened it to find Lord Carew standing there looking like Satan himself come to tempt her.

"I thought," he began, his voice quieter than usual, "that you might wish to watch as we approach Kenmare Bay. 'Tis a sight worth seeing."

Grace blinked in surprise, her heart leaping before she could suppress it. "Oh. Yes, I would very much like that. Thank you."

He stepped aside, allowing her to follow him on to the deck. The crisp, bracing morning air greeted her, carrying with it the familiar tang of salt and something else—something earthy and green. Ireland. They were nearly there.

As she reached the railing, the horizon was no longer the endless expanse of sea she had grown accustomed to. Instead, it was broken by cliffs, their rugged faces rising dramatically from the water. The sunlight danced across their surfaces, as though nature herself had carved out the stone.

The cliffs gave way to rolling hills, their slopes lush with emerald grass that glowed in the sunlight. Scattered dots of white hinted at cottages, their thatched roofs contrasting with the verdant landscape. It was a place both wild and welcoming, untamed yet not. Grace felt a pang of longing she could not explain, as though some part of it called to her like England's gentle countryside.

As the ship rounded a bend in the coast, a medieval castle came into view, perched high above the bay. Its imposing silhouette proclaimed it a fortress with its towers and turrets, while the wide windows reflected light. The castle commanded its position with authority over the water and the cliffs, where waves crashed against the rocks below. It was stunning, a place to warn off invaders and make them question the wisdom of trying to attack.

"That is your home?" Grace asked, her voice awe-filled.

Carew nodded. "Donnellan Castle." There was a note of pride in his tone, tempered by something quieter—perhaps even wistfulness.

"It's…magnificent. I do not think I could have conjured such beauty in my dreams," she said earnestly, her eyes sweeping over the house and its surroundings. "Though it looks fierce at the same time."

He chuckled softly, a sound that sent warmth through her chest. "An intentional impression, and there's some truth in it. I love that the cliffs have always shaped the castle as much as the castle has shaped the land."

She turned her attention back to the view, allowing the silence between them to stretch, comfortable and companionable.

As the ship drew closer to the bay, the details of Donnellan came into sharper clarity—the tall stone walls, rising from the cliffs down which water poured in a great fall into the sea below. Grace could scarcely take it all in.

And yet, as much as she looked forward to setting foot on land, to exploring the castle and its grounds, a quiet sadness settled over her. This journey, this time with Carew, had been a gift she had never expected. She feared that once they disembarked, the spell would be broken, and he would retreat into his revenge on Flynn, leaving her on the periphery once more.

"Miss Whitford," Carew said suddenly, drawing her attention back to him. There was something in his expression she could not quite place, a flicker of hesitation. "I hope you will find Donnellan to your liking."

"I am certain I will," she replied, her heart tinged with sadness. "It is an extraordinary place, my lord."

"I wish I would be able to show it to you." His gaze lingered on her for a moment longer, as though he wished to say more, but then he turned back to the view, thus putting a jagged point on any question she might have had about furthering their relationship. If what this was could be quantified as such.

Grace followed his lead, and turned to watch as the ship made its final approach.

The cliffs seemed to rise higher as they entered the bay, the waves gentler now, lapping against the ship's sides with a rhythm that matched the beating of her heart. For better or worse, their journey was coming to an end, and with it the fragile connection she had begun to treasure. Her insides felt stripped bare, as though the pages of her fairy tale were ripped away—ended before it had really begun.

Perhaps she needed to read less. Her flair for dramatic prose, even if only in her thoughts, was startling.

A loud crack sounded, sharp and jarring, breaking the tranquillity like a thunderclap. Grace started, clutching the railing as the ship jolted with the impact of something striking its hull. Shouts erupted around her, the crew scrambling to action, their movements swift and purposeful. Another crack followed, splintering a section of the deck not far from where she stood. It was only then that she realised the ship was under attack.

"Get down!" a voice commanded, cutting through the chaos like steel through silk. Before she could fully comprehend what was happening, she felt the solid weight of Lord Carew pressing her down to the deck, his arm shielding her head as another deafening crack split the air. She barely registered the shouts of the crew or the distant flash of gunfire. All of her senses were centred on the protective presence of Carew, his body taut with tension, his breath steady despite the danger.

"Do not move until I tell you," he instructed, his voice calm but firm.

Her heart hammered in her chest, the shock of the moment rendering her mute. She nodded, her cheek pressed against the rough wood of the deck as the acrid smell of gunpowder filled her nose. Carew shifted slightly, his sharp gaze sweeping across the horizon as if assessing the threat.

"They've positioned themselves along the cliffs. A coward's tactic."

Grace clung to his words, her mind reeling. Who would dare fire upon them? It must be Flynn's doing. Had the enmity between the families escalated to open violence? She did not know, and in that moment, she could not bring herself to ask. Her world had narrowed to the immediate danger and the steady presence of Carew beside her.

Another shot struck the ship, the sound reverberating through the planks beneath them, followed by a sickening cackle of laughter that echoed through the cove.

Carew shifted again, his hand brushing hers as he steadied himself. "We're almost there," he said, his tone unwavering. "They'll not sink us with rifles."

The confidence in his voice was a lifeline, and Grace clung to it, drawing strength from his certainty. The ship's crew worked with desperate efficiency, steering the vessel towards the safety of the Donnellan dock. The cliffs loomed larger now, the enemy fire becoming less frequent as the ship moved beyond their reach.

When the ship finally turned a corner and docked, the gunfire ceased, leaving only the rush of the sea and the shouts of the crew to fill the air. Carew rose slowly, his hand extending to help Grace to her feet. She grasped it, her legs unsteady but her resolve firm. She could not falter now.

∼

RONAN HAD to leave his well-trained crew to see to the mooring of the ship once they reached the protected alcove where *The Selkie* rested.

His primary concern was escorting Grace safely off the ship and into the castle.

Flynn's hand was in this—of that, he had no doubt. The shots fired upon their arrival were not an attempt to sink them but a warning, a reckless message meant for him, whether Flynn had fired himself or left his minions with orders to terrorize. What was Flynn's purpose? And why now? Ronan did not think the man so foolish as to resort to outright murder, at least not yet. But Grace…

His gaze flicked towards the cliffs, their rugged heights climbing into the sky, and then towards the sheltered stairway carved into the rock—a steep, winding path that would lead him home to the castle. It was a long climb, but the stairs through the cliffs were protected.

Home. The word carried a weight he could not quite name. He had always thought of Donnellan and its austere beauty as a refuge, a place of stability. Yet, today, as he prepared to ascend those familiar steps, unease settled heavily in his chest. Flynn had never attacked them directly, nor during the day, nor so close to home.

His jaw tightened as his gaze shifted to Grace. She stood a few paces away, her head tilted upwards slightly as she took in the sight of the cliffs and the castle rising above them. Her wide eyes held a mixture of wonder and apprehension, a response that stirred something unexpected within him. He had grown accustomed to the stark beauty of the place, its commanding presence on the coast. But seeing it through her eyes made him pause. Did she see more than stone and mortar? Did she see perhaps even something unspoken in its proud edifice?

As he led her quickly across the gangway to safety, his heart hardened as his mind turned back to the man who threatened to destroy all Ronan held dear. The long-standing feud between their families had deep roots, its origins obscured by years of bitterness and mistrust. Yet Flynn seemed determined not merely to perpetuate the feud but to escalate it, to strike at the very heart of his family. To what purpose? Was there more beneath the surface that Ronan could not see?

It was hard to fathom such malice, though he had seen glimpses of its effects—his mother's frayed nerves, Maeve's growing restlessness. Flynn's influence was spreading like a shadow, and now it had reached even these cliffs, the last place Ronan had thought it could touch. Flynn's boldness had grown, and Ronan feared if he didn't stop it now, it would pervade like a spreading disease. Something that infests before you know how bad it is.

The climb up the stairs was arduous but familiar. The carved stone steps wound through the cliffs, sheltered by a narrow tunnel lit by lanterns. Grace followed behind him, her steps careful but determined, and he could not help but glance back occasionally to ensure her safety. At last, the final step brought them to the top, where Donnellan Castle stood waiting.

Its weathered stone walls loomed large, the iron gates creaking open as a servant rushed to greet them.

It was home, and yet something felt amiss. He saw it in the hurried steps of the servants, the unease in their glances as they passed. He wished he knew what he was walking into. Had his father taken a turn—or worse?

His mother was waiting in the great hall. Lady Donnellan, always a figure of composure, now appeared anything but. Her gown was slightly askew, her hair escaping its pins, and her face bore the strain of sleepless nights. She turned to Ronan the moment he entered, her expression one of desperation and relief all at once.

"Ronan," she began, her voice trembling. "Thank God you are here."

"What has happened?" he asked, his tone sharp with concern. "Why is the household in such disarray?"

"It's Maeve," Lady Eleanor said, clutching his arm. "She is gone."

"Gone?" The word felt foreign, its implications too vast to grasp. "What do you mean, gone?"

His mother's grip tightened. "That rogue has cast his spell on her, Ronan. I tried to stop it, but she...she believes herself in love with him. She has eloped with him. I found a note this morning."

The room seemed to tilt slightly, the weight of her words crashing over him like a wave. Maeve. His sister, spirited and trusting, had fallen prey to Flynn's manipulations. Fury surged within him, hot and unrelenting, though he kept his expression carefully composed.

"Does Father know?" The knowledge would be the final nail in his coffin.

His mother shook her head with a look that indicated worry over her decision not to tell him. She had aged since he'd left only two months ago. "I was afraid of what it would do to him."

"Do we know where they have gone?" he asked, his voice low but dangerous.

His mother shook her head, tears glistening in her eyes. "No. They could be anywhere by now. I have sent men after them, but there has been no word."

Ronan's fists clenched at his sides, his mind racing. Flynn's audacity knew no bounds. To lure Maeve away, to use her as a pawn in his twisted game—this was beyond enmity. It was war.

"I will find her," he said, his voice hard. "I will bring her back."

His mother placed a trembling hand on his cheek. "Ronan, you must be careful. Flynn…he is not like other men. I fear what he might do if cornered."

"I know what he is, Mother," Ronan replied, his tone steely. "And I know what must be done. I will not let Flynn destroy Maeve—or this family."

He glanced at Grace then, her presence a quiet reminder of the other dangers he had faced to reach this point. She stood near the doorway, her expression unreadable but her eyes steady on his. She had just seen Flynn's darkness, too, had felt its reach if only on the surface. Ronan knew he could not afford to falter now—not for Maeve, not for his family, and not for the future he was only beginning to imagine.

Amidst all of this, Ronan turned towards Grace, his feelings softening slightly despite the storm of emotions raging within him. "Mother," he said, his voice steadier now, "may I introduce Miss Grace Whitford? She has been my companion on this journey, though I regret to say under circumstances neither of us anticipated." His gaze flicked briefly to Grace, as if willing her to understand his haste. "I am afraid I must leave her to recount the details of how she comes to be here. She has endured much, and I trust you will see to her comfort in my absence." His words were formal, but the glance he gave his mother carried an unspoken plea for care, a rare moment of vulnerability that his mother did not miss.

Her brows lifted ever so slightly as Ronan finished speaking. For a fleeting moment, she said nothing, her keen eyes shifting from Ronan to Grace. He had little doubt she was taking in the younger woman's slightly rumpled but dignified appearance, and then she regarded Ronan with an expression that was equal parts curiosity and concern. Despite the surprise evident in her features, she stepped forward with a grace that belied the weariness Ronan knew she must feel.

"This is unexpected, even for you, Ronan." Her lips curved faintly, though the gesture held more curiosity than amusement. She turned her attention fully to Grace, inclining her head with a graciousness that made Grace's posture relax ever so slightly. "Miss Whitford, welcome to Donnellan Castle. I trust you will find our home a refuge after what I can only imagine has been a trying journey. I apologize that things are not well here, as you must know."

Grace dipped into a small curtsy. "It is I who must beg your forgiveness, Lady Donnellan, for imposing upon your household so unexpectedly and at such a time."

Lady Donnellan waved her hand dismissively, a gracious smile softening her features. "Nonsense, my dear. You are most welcome here. Perhaps," she added with a touch of shrewdness, "you can be of some comfort to me whilst Ronan finds Maeve and explain how this all came to pass."

Ronan kissed his mother's cheek, and he was filled with gratitude. "Thank you, Mother. I knew I could rely on you."

With a nod, Ronan turned back to Grace. "I will return as soon as I can," he said quietly. "You will be safe here."

Grace offered him a faint, understanding smile, though her eyes betrayed a flicker of unease. "Go," she said softly.

With a deep breath, he turned back to his mother. "I must prepare to leave at once."

CHAPTER 12

The ship's deck tilted slightly as *The Tempest* drew closer to the Irish coast, the breeze carrying the distinct tang of salt and earth mingling on the air. Joy gripped the railing, her knuckles white with tension as she scanned the distant shore. The cliffs of Ireland rose jagged and proud against the horizon, their rugged beauty not lost on her as she fretted over the purpose of their journey.

Now that they were finally there, the reality that they might find Grace very changed did nothing to ease the knot in Joy's chest.

"Will she be different?" Joy wondered quietly, though loud enough for her sister to hear.

Patience glanced up from where she had been adjusting her bonnet. Her expression, equal parts concern and resolve, mirrored Joy's sentiments. "I do not know, my dear. It is possible she may have been through a very trying time," Patience replied. "But mayhap we will find her delighted with her adventure, none the worse for a week on her own."

Joy knew her face must mirror her thoughts, which were full of doubt. Her imaginings, which were very colourful, had conjured her sister fighting off pirates and sea monsters.

Freddy sat on a barrel nearby, cradling Evalina. The little creature purred contentedly as he stroked her soft fur. "Perhaps Grace is even now enjoying a pleasant journey, unaware of our concern."

Joy shook her head. "I cannot imagine she is at ease, not with all that has transpired." The group fell into a contemplative silence, each lost in their own thoughts about what they would soon face. The sea rolled gently around them, the waves glinting under the midday sun. Seagulls circled overhead, their cries echoing in the open air.

As late afternoon approached, the distant outline of civilization began to emerge. Joy's heart quickened at the sight. "Look!" she exclaimed, pointing ahead. "We are nearly there."

Patience stepped forward, her gaze intent. "At last. We must prepare to disembark as swiftly as possible."

As *The Tempest* drew closer to shore, the details of the coast became clearer. The cliffs rose sharp and rugged, contrasting with the smoother water. Sitting atop one of the cliffs was an imposing castle —its stone walls bathed in the warm hues of the setting sun. This must be what the Castle of Athlin was like from Radcliffe's story set in the Highlands, Joy mused.

The Kenmare harbour bustled with activity as *The Tempest* docked, the sounds of shouting sailors, creaking ropes, and seagulls mingling in the air. Joy practically leaped from the gangplank the moment it was secured, barely able to contain her energy. Patience followed more deliberately, her hand resting lightly on Ashley's arm as they descended. Freddy brought up the rear, Evalina peering curiously from inside his waistcoat.

Ashley had efficiently secured a carriage, and soon they were winding their way along the coastal road towards the castle. Joy gazed out of the window, feeling her eyes widening with fascination as she watched the sheep graze to one side and water cascade down cliffs on the other.

The towering castle came into view as the sun shone late in the sky, now casting long shadows across the landscape. As the carriage pulled up to the front entrance, a young footman rushed forward to greet them. "Please forgive the delay," he said breathlessly, helping the ladies down. "His lordship is preparing to leave."

"Leave?" Joy repeated, alarmed. "Where is he going?"

"To pursue Lady Maeve," the footman explained, his tone hushed as though speaking the words aloud might deepen the scandal.

The group exchanged grim looks of confusion before stepping inside. They were met by a stern-looking butler who eyed them with a mixture of curiosity and wariness.

"Good evening," Ashley began politely. "We are here to see Lord Carew. It is a matter of some importance."

The butler hesitated. "His lordship is occupied at present. There has been—"

"Please," Joy interjected, her tone imploring. "We are searching for our sister, Miss Grace Whitford. We believe she may be here."

At the mention of Grace's name, the butler's posture relaxed a little. "Ah, yes. Miss Whitford is indeed a guest of the house."

Relief washed over Joy, nearly buckling her knees. "May we see her?"

"Of course. If you would kindly wait in the drawing room, I shall inform her of your arrival."

They were ushered inside, the grandeur of the interior momentarily overshadowed for Joy by their collective concern. As they settled into the elegant room, she could scarcely sit still, her fingers scratching beneath Evalina's chin now that she had pried her from Freddy.

Moments later, the door opened, and Grace entered, her eyes widening in surprise at the sight of her sisters and friends. "Joy! Patience! Ashley! Freddy!" she exclaimed, rushing forward to embrace them.

"Grace, thank heaven," Joy breathed, holding her tightly. "We have been so worried."

Grace pulled back slightly, a faint blush colouring her cheeks. "I am sorry to have caused you distress. It was all rather unexpected."

"The blame is mine! Can you forgive me?"

Grace, never one to hold a grudge, hugged Joy to reassure her. The relief was immense. "I am quite well, Joy."

Patience regarded Grace carefully, as though she sensed a change in Grace. "Has Lord Carew treated you kindly?"

"Yes, of course," Grace assured them. "He has been most considerate."

Joy smiled warmly. "I am relieved to hear it. And what of the journey? Was it very dreadful?"

Grace hesitated. "There were…complications. But I am safe now. There are far more worrisome happenings occurring here…"

"Lady Maeve is missing?" Joy offered.

Grace looked at her sister with surprise.

"A footman let it slip." She gave a slight shrug of her shoulder—the type her governess was forever saying wasn't ladylike.

"Mr. Flynn convinced her to elope with him."

Before they could enquire further, the door opened again, and Lord Carew himself entered. His demeanour was grave, his eyes shadowed with concern.

"Miss Whitford," he began, then stopped upon noticing the others. "Ah, your family has come to rescue you." Joy didn't think he sounded relieved. Curious.

Ashley stepped forward, extending his hand. "Carew. I must thank you for the unexpected care of Miss Grace."

Joy wasted no time: with one adventure completed, on to the next. "But what of Maeve? Who is Flynn?"

Carew's jaw clenched. "The worst sort of scoundrel. He lured my sister away under the guise of an elopement. It appears she went willingly, but I will find her, and I will bring her back."

Ashley stepped forward. "We are at your disposal."

Carew inclined his head. "Your assistance is appreciated, Major, but I must warn you, Flynn is no ordinary scoundrel. He does not play or fight like a gentleman."

"We understand the risks," Ashley said firmly. "But this is no time for caution. If Lady Maeve is with him, every moment counts."

"I have just sent my crew back out to search the bay. I'm headed for Corlach Keep to see if he has taken her there."

"He will feel safest there," Stuart agreed.

"The fastest way is across the bay, but that is how he expects us to come after him. We will be easy targets in the water. I did not feel comfortable sending my men back out, but I need them there to prevent him trying to escape with her that way. The ba—scoundrel fired shots at us as we approached."

Joy, who had been standing near the window, spun around, her eyes wide with alarm. "Shots? He fired at you? At Grace?" she exclaimed, her voice rising involuntarily with her worry and outrage. "That vile, cowardly—"

~

"She was not harmed," Ronan said quickly, though the tension in his voice betrayed his own fears. "Yes, it shows how far Flynn is willing to go. He is vile and dangerous."

"He has no right—no right to do any of this!"

Ronan looked amused at Joy's tenacity despite the seriousness of the situation.

"How long has she been gone?" Stuart directed them back to the task at hand.

"Since sometime during the night. The man doesn't keep his word. I was to have had two more days."

Stuart whistled under his breath. "And if he has her at his home?"

"It is a fortress much like this one. These castles along the water were built to withstand Norman invaders and the like."

"Do you suggest we sneak in and steal her away? Or knock on the door and ask politely?" Stuart asked with a hint of sarcasm.

"Unfortunately, the gloves are off. He knows I will come after her, and very likely has set traps."

Stuart folded his arms and regarded Ronan thoughtfully. "How many men does Flynn have? If we are to succeed in this, we need a clear understanding of what we are up against. Numbers, their positions—anything you can give me. If we are to act, we act with precision."

Ronan appreciated Stuart's sharp military mind, but the question still sent a grim tension through him. "Flynn has at least two dozen loyal men, maybe more," Ronan replied. "They are not disciplined soldiers, but they're cutthroats and pirates who enjoy fighting dirty. The terrain works to his advantage as well. His estate is surrounded by rocky cliffs and narrow paths—easy to defend, difficult to infiltrate."

"We will need more than sheer numbers. Strategy is key. If it is a fortress, we need to anticipate where his men might be stationed. Guard rotations, blind spots. Do you have any idea of what sort of traps he might set?"

"Flynn thrives on manipulation and misdirection," Ronan said darkly. "He will use whatever he can—false surrenders, hidden ambushes. He's not above taking the most underhanded approach if it means gaining the upper hand."

Stuart nodded his understanding. "It won't be my first battle, but I cannot like for the ladies to be involved."

"There is power in numbers. He cannot kill all of us. I will not be left behind," Patience declared.

"If Maeve is in danger, I wish to help. And she will need comfort while you deal with Flynn," Grace added.

Carew regarded her for a moment, his expression inscrutable. Finally, he sighed. "Very well. But you will follow my orders. I will not risk your safety further."

Ashley clapped a hand on Carew's shoulder. "Then let us waste no more time. The longer Flynn has, the harder it will be to catch him."

Preparations were swift, the household in a flurry of activity as horses were readied and provisions packed. Lady Donnellan appeared briefly, her face drawn with worry as she bid her son farewell. "Bring her back," she implored, her voice trembling. "Bring Maeve home."

"I will, Mother," Carew promised, his voice low but firm.

As the party mounted their horses and rode out into the gathering dusk, the wind carried the faint scent of the sea, mingling with the promise of impending conflict. The road ahead was fraught with uncertainty, but one thing was clear: they would stop at nothing to save Maeve and thwart Flynn's schemes.

CHAPTER 13

Cool, sharp air carried the tang of salt and the earthy dampness of the Irish countryside as the search party set out from Donnellan Castle. The group pressed onward, their horses' hooves pounding rhythmically against the packed earthen road that wound its way around the edges of Kenmare Bay. Overhead, the moon hung bright and commanding, its pale light casting long, eerie shadows across the landscape.

Grace couldn't help but think of those times aboard *The Selkie*, how the stars had seemed brighter, closer somehow, as if she could reach up and touch them. The ship had been a place of strange magic —her quiet conversations with Carew, the moments when his gaze had softened, and she had glimpsed something warmer beneath his practised exterior. Those memories seemed so far away now, almost as if they belonged to another lifetime.

Tonight, however, the world felt stark and unforgiving. The rugged beauty of the land, with its wild cliffs and shadowed glens, offered no solace. Every mile they covered brought them closer to Corlach Keep, and closer to what unknown awaited them there.

Grace found herself riding alongside Carew, though he seemed distant, his attention fixed resolutely ahead. His shoulders were stiff, his jaw tight, and the camaraderie they had shared on the ship was absent. She wanted to say something, to erase his worries and bring back the ease that had grown between them on the ship, but the words wouldn't come. Instead, she rode in silence, her thoughts churning as the moonlit road stretched endlessly before them.

Finally, she mustered the courage to break the silence. "What will you do if Maeve does not want to come back?" she asked, her voice tentative but steady.

Carew's head turned slightly, though he didn't look at her directly. For a moment, he didn't respond, the tension in his profile stark in the pale light. When he finally spoke, his voice was low and measured. "Then she does not understand what she has chosen, and will be made to see in time."

His reply unsettled her. "Supposing she believes she loves him?" Grace pressed gently. "She may think she is doing the right thing."

Carew's jaw tightened further, his tone hardening. "I am certain she believes it, else she would not have gone off with him, but that doesn't make it true. Flynn is not capable of love—not the kind that Maeve deserves. He uses people, manipulates them to serve his own ends. I will not allow her to be one of his pawns."

She already is, Grace thought with a frown, her chest tightening with the weight of his words. She had no love for Flynn, that much was certain, but she could not dismiss the possibility that Maeve might have genuine feelings for the man, however misguided. The thought of Maeve's heartbreak, should those feelings be torn apart, would create a divide that would be difficult to repair again. "But if she resists…" Grace began, only for Carew to cut her off.

"Then I will convince her," he said firmly, his tone brooking no argument. "Whatever it takes, I will bring her back."

The finality in his voice left little room for discussion, and Grace fell silent, her gaze drifting to the landscape around them. The moonlit hills and valleys seemed vast and indifferent, their beauty tinged with an ominous sense of foreboding. She shivered slightly, though only partly from the chill night.

Behind her, she could hear the murmur of conversation between the others. Joy's voice, lyrical but determined, carried over the steady rhythm of the horses' hooves, occasionally arguing good-naturedly with Freddy. Patience and Ashley rode close together, their silhouettes a picture of quiet strength and unity.

As the hours dragged on, her body began to ache from the unrelenting pace, but she refused to complain. The urgency of their mission left no room for weakness. The moon had climbed higher in the sky, its light growing colder and more distant, when they finally crested a hill that offered a sweeping view of Kenmare Bay.

The bay glittered like molten silver, its surface rippling gently under the moonlight. The land around it was wild and untamed, dotted with the dark shapes of trees and the occasional flicker of a distant lantern. In the distance, perched on the edge of a rugged promontory, was Flynn's own medieval castle—a forbidding silhouette against the night sky.

"There it is," Carew said grimly, his voice cutting through the quiet. He reined in his horse, the others following suit, as he surveyed the keep with an intensity that made Grace's stomach twist.

"How do you wish to proceed?" Ashley asked, his tone brisk and authoritative.

Carew's gaze remained fixed on the stone fortress.

"We will approach cautiously. Reconnoitre. I doubt Flynn will expect us tonight, but we cannot assume he is unprepared. He did greet *The Selkie's* arrival, after all."

"If at all possible, we need to find Maeve and get her out before Flynn has a chance to interfere." Ashley had the most experience with these types of operations.

The task was daunting, and as Grace stood with the others, gazing at the imposing stone fortress, she finally grasped the magnitude of what lay before them. Similar to Donnellan, its high walls and narrow, arrow-slit windows spoke of centuries of defiance, a place meant to repel invaders and safeguard its secrets. It was not a welcoming sight. Grace, for all her imagination, could not picture any but a medieval army with flaming arrows and catapults managing to breach it.

The air around their small party was charged with tension as they huddled together in the shadow of a nearby grove, their voices low and cautious.

"We should surround it," Carew said, his tone clipped and authoritative. His dark gaze was fixed on the fortress, every muscle in his body coiled with determination. "Positioning ourselves near all entrances is essential. There could well be an escape tunnel we cannot see."

Grace nodded, her thoughts briefly straying to the stories she had read. Hidden tunnels and secret passageways were staples of the novels she adored, and they had a believability about them. She could almost imagine Flynn slinking away through some dark, damp passage, his shadowy figure disappearing into the cliffs.

Ashley leaned forward, his brow furrowed in thought. "We need to get someone inside," he said. "If we rely on watching, we might be here for weeks with nothing to show for it. Flynn will know how to hide—if he even brought her here."

Carew considered this, his expression grim. "Perhaps a servant could be bribed," he conceded, though his tone suggested distaste for the idea.

"It is worth trying," Ashley agreed. He glanced at his wife. "Patience and I can take that entrance," he added, gesturing towards a smaller gate on the eastern side of the stone wall.

Grace, who had been listening intently, suddenly felt a spark of determination. A plan began to take shape in her mind, one that seemed as daring as it was logical. She hesitated for only a moment before speaking. "I shall go to the front door, looking for shelter," she said, her voice steady.

The effect of her words was immediate. The entire group turned to her, their expressions a mixture of disbelief, astonishment, and doubt. Joy, however, looked at her with something akin to admiration, a spark of encouragement in her sharp eyes.

"Nay, lass," Carew said after a moment, his tone firm. "I'll not have you go alone. You do not understand what this man is capable of."

Grace met his gaze without flinching. "Perhaps not fully," she admitted, "but I understand enough. He has no quarrel with me, and as I am unknown to him, I do not believe he would find me suspicious. I am unassuming, unremarkable. They would not refuse me shelter."

Carew's eyes narrowed. "This is no jest. Flynn is dangerous."

"I know," Grace said quietly, "but this may be our best chance. He will not suspect me, and I can gather information. Perhaps I may even locate Maeve."

Ashley looked at her closely, weighing her words. "It's a bold plan," he admitted, "but it's not without risk."

"All plans carry risk," Grace countered. "If you have a better idea, I shall gladly step aside."

Patience reached out to touch Ashley's arm, her expression thoughtful. "She may be right," she said softly. Then she turned to Carew and said, "A stranger asking for shelter on a cold night is far less suspicious than you pounding on the front door demanding to see your sister."

Carew turned away, his jaw tightening as he studied the fortress. The flicker of torchlight on the walls seemed to mock their indecision. Finally, he sighed and turned back to Grace.

"If you insist on doing this," he said reluctantly, "you must have an escape plan. I will stay close to the door, ready to intervene if anything goes wrong."

Grace inclined her head, accepting his condition. "Very well, but I must appear to be alone when I approach."

Carew stared at her, his expression dark. "This is reckless."

"Yet necessary," Grace said, her voice steady. She held his gaze directly, unwavering. "Do you trust me?"

For a moment, he said nothing. Then, with a reluctant nod, he answered. "I do, but I do not wish to risk you as well."

"Then you must let me do this."

With the plan agreed upon, Grace felt a strange mixture of fear and resolve settle over her. The fortress was no less daunting, the risks no less grave, but for the first time, she felt like more than an observer in this ordeal. She had a part to play, and she would see it to its conclusion.

As they began their descent towards the keep, Grace mustered her courage. She would finally do something adventurous like her sisters. Perhaps she could be brave, she just needed the right cause.

∼

RONAN RODE at the head of their party, Grace alongside him like a silent sentinel. She should not be here, of course, but resistance to the Whitford charm—or force—seemed impossible. It was a peculiar spell they cast, one that ensnared even the strongest of wills. Westwood, Rotham, Stuart—each had succumbed in their turn, and now it was his own resolve that faltered, no matter how fiercely he tried to guard his heart.

There was comfort, however, in her presence. Despite the risks, her calm strength steadied him, supporting him against the tumult of his thoughts. As they made their final descent through the darkened hillside, her quiet determination reminded him that he was not alone in this battle. Yet the thought of her venturing into Flynn's den set his nerves alight with equal parts of dread and frustration. Why had he allowed her to convince him? Why had he not insisted on a safer plan?

An eerie mist clung to the ground along their path. The moonlight rendered the scene both ethereal and menacing, every shadow a potential hiding place for an unseen enemy. Ronan's mind turned to the possibility of sharpshooters, though he hoped the element of surprise and cover of darkness was on his side. Flynn was cunning, but he preferred to play games, where his charm and guile could work their full effect. Still, Ronan's hand rested lightly on the butt of his pistol, his senses attuned to every sound in the stillness.

Every twist and turn of the path brought them closer to Flynn's door, closer to Maeve—and closer to the confrontation that had been years in the making. The anticipation was a slow-burning fire in his chest, its heat stoked by a potent mix of anger, guilt, and dread.

It was hard for Ronan not to dwell on the many ways he might make Flynn suffer once he had him in his grasp. The man had crossed every boundary of decency, weaving his poisonous charm into the heart of one too trusting to see him for what he was. That Maeve, Ronan's own sister, had fallen prey to Flynn's lies was a betrayal he could scarcely fathom. She was young, full of idealistic hope that peace might be achieved where bitterness had long reigned. Flynn had exploited that hope with ruthless precision.

Ronan's jaw tightened as his thoughts spiralled into darker themes. He pictured Flynn's smug smirk, his casual arrogance as he led Maeve away. A duel would be too honourable, too swift for the likes of him. Flynn deserved the weight of every moment of suffering he had caused, and Ronan would see to it personally.

When they finally crested the last rise, Corlach Keep came back into view, its dark outline imposing against the night sky. Torchlight marked the perimeter, a reminder of the men stationed there under Flynn's command. Ronan reined in his horse and motioned for the others to stop.

"This is as far as we go on horseback," he said quietly, his voice firm. He turned to Grace, who dismounted with quiet efficiency. Her face was pale but determined, her hands steady as she adjusted her cloak.

"You know the plan," Ronan continued, his eyes locking with hers. "You go to the door and ask for shelter. Once inside, you must find Maeve and convince her to leave with you. If anything goes wrong—anything at all—you signal, and we will find a way in."

Grace nodded, her gaze unwavering. "I understand."

Ronan hesitated, the weight of what he was asking pressing heavily on him. "Flynn is dangerous," he said, his voice low. "Do not trust anything he says."

"I won't," she replied softly. "I am hoping to avoid him altogether, but I know not to trust him. He is nothing like you."

Her words struck in a way he hadn't expected, and for a brief moment, he wavered in letting her do this. He wanted to tell her to stop, to stay behind where it was safe, but he knew he needed her. Grace Whitford was determined and capable. How wrong he'd been about her. The fact was, he needed her, and she could do what he could not.

He watched as she moved across the old drawbridge, her figure a shadow against the mist-laden ground. The sound of her boots on the path was deafening to Ronan, though he knew it was his anxiety for Grace's safety. He forced himself to remain still, though every instinct screamed for him to stop her, to bring her back. He stayed in the shadows, his gaze never leaving her.

When she reached the heavy wooden door, she paused for a moment before lifting the iron knocker and letting it fall with a resounding thud that reverberated through the night.

The seconds stretched into what felt like hours before the door creaked open. A man appeared, his face indiscernible against the faint light from within. Ronan couldn't hear their words, but he saw Grace's posture—calm, unthreatening, utterly convincing. The man seemed to hesitate, then stepped aside, allowing her entry. As the door closed behind her, Ronan felt an unfamiliar panic.

She was inside Flynn's lair now, and there was nothing he could do to protect her. The thought was like a knife twisting in his gut. Not only was his sister under Flynn's roof, but now Grace—the woman who had somehow managed to crack the armour around his heart—was there as well. His mind raced with questions. Would Grace find Maeve? Would his sister trust this stranger and agree to leave? Or would Flynn's influence prove too strong?

Ronan was coiled as tight as a spring, ready to explode. He replayed the plan over and over in his mind, searching for flaws, for anything they might have overlooked. He had always prided himself on his ability to anticipate every possible outcome, but now, as he waited in the shadows, he realized how much of their success was beyond his control.

If anything happened to Grace, he would never forgive himself.

Stuart's voice, low and steady, broke through his thoughts. "She's strong, Carew. And clever. She will find a way. We are setting off to the servants' entrance."

Ronan nodded curtly, though his throat felt tight. He didn't trust himself to speak. His gaze remained fixed on the door, afraid to miss any sign of trouble within.

If Flynn thought he could take what mattered most to Ronan and walk away unscathed, he was sorely mistaken. Flynn would pay.

Ronan stood alone just beyond the door of the keep, his body coiled with tension, every muscle taut. His ears strained for the slightest sound, his eyes fixed on the shadowy silhouette of the castle against the moonlit sky. He had never realized, but the sheer helplessness of waiting was worse than being flayed alive. All he could do was wait.

Grace was inside, braving the lion's den with nothing but her wits and her courage. The memory of her determination, the quiet resolve in her eyes, was both a source of pride and torment.

Every creak of the bridge, every animal noise drifting on the wind set his heart pounding. He imagined the worst—Flynn discovering her, Grace caught in a trap, Maeve too frightened or injured to escape. The possibilities played out endlessly in his mind, each more dire than the last. He whispered a curse under his breath. If anything happened to her, he would never forgive himself.

He scanned the walls again, he searched for any sign of movement, any signal that Grace had found Maeve and was making her way out. The shadows seemed alive, shifting and writhing with every flicker of moonlight.

The waiting was agony, a torment that gnawed at his composure. Every minute felt like a lifetime. He prided himself on his ability to remain calm under pressure, to act with precision and control even in the most chaotic of circumstances. But this was different. This was Grace. This was Maeve. The stakes were not just his own life, but the lives of the two women he cared for most in the world.

A faint sound reached his ears—a distant creak of wood, perhaps a door opening or closing. He held his breath, leaning forward, his eyes narrowing as he tried to discern its source. Was it them? Or had Flynn's men discovered her?

"Come on, Grace," he whispered, his voice barely audible. "Come back to me."

The thought of losing her, of failing his sister, was a weight he could scarcely bear. Yet beneath the fear and the anguish was a flicker of hope, a belief that Grace's strength and ingenuity would see her through this ordeal. All he could do was trust her—and be ready to act the moment she emerged.

CHAPTER 14

The door creaked open, and a servant with a stooping posture and wary eyes peered out, the faint glow of a wall sconce behind him casting flickering shadows across his lined face. Grace adjusted her cloak, feigning the hesitation of a weary traveller caught unprepared by the cold and dark.

"Please, sir," she said, her voice soft and steady, "I have lost my way and seek shelter for the night. I would be most grateful if you might grant me a place to rest until morning."

The servant squinted at Grace, his suspicion evident as he took her measure. "And what's an English lass doing wandering the Irish countryside at this hour? This isn't a place for the likes of you."

Grace offered a weary smile, her cloak pulled tight around her. "I assure you, sir, I am no threat. My party was separated during our journey to Kenmare, and I have been trying to find my way back ever since. The storm last night left me disoriented, and I have not seen a soul for hours. Please, I only seek shelter until morning."

The servant hesitated, his stern expression wavering at her explanation. "Kenmare, you say?" he muttered, scratching at his temple. "That's quite the journey for someone on foot."

"It is," Grace agreed, letting a note of exhaustion creep into her voice. "And one I would not have undertaken had I had any other choice. Surely you would not turn away someone who has nowhere else to go?"

After a long pause, the man grumbled under his breath but stepped aside, his gaze sweeping over her before nodding curtly. "The master does not usually take to unexpected guests," he muttered, stepping aside, "but I'll not have it said we turned a lady into the night."

"Thank you, sir." Grace inclined her head and stepped over the threshold, her boots echoing against the stone floor. The entry was dimly lit with torch sconces, its high ceiling vaulted with wooden beams. Cold drafts of air carried the faint scent of damp stone and old wood. The walls were adorned with faded tapestries that told of ghosts in their former glory.

"This way," the servant murmured, leading her up the stairs, then down a narrow corridor. The castle seemed to slumber, its occupants unaware of her presence—or so she hoped. She'd lost track of what hour it was.

They reached a small room near the end of the hall. The servant opened the door, revealing a sparse but serviceable space: a low bed with a woollen blanket, a single chair by the hearth, and a small table holding a half-burned candle.

"You may rest here," the man said, setting the candle alight with his own. "I'll bring water if you need it."

"That will not be necessary," Grace replied with a grateful smile. "Thank you."

He nodded, retreating and closing the door behind him. Grace stood still for a moment, listening intently as his footsteps receded down the corridor. The flickering candle cast a warm glow, but it did little to dispel the oppressive atmosphere of the castle. She had entered the enemy's lair, and every fibre of her being was alert to the danger that surrounded her.

Her heart fluttered like a trapped bird, and her palms were clammy with fear. Grace had never done anything like this before, and most of her wanted to turn back and flee the castle. But she was so close to finding Maeve, she could not let Carew down. She must find her courage!

There was no time to waste, so she considered her next move. If Maeve was here, she must be found before the household stirred and Grace's presence was discovered.

She extinguished the candle, plunging the room into darkness. After allowing her eyes to adjust, she quietly opened the door and peered into the corridor.

The dim sconces lining the walls cast long, flickering shadows that made her jump, and her heart hammered louder with every step she took along the labyrinth of halls. Each creak of the floorboards felt deafening, and every faint rustle of fabric sent her spinning to check for someone ready to shout that she was an intruder.

She reached the central staircase, its stone steps spiralling upward into the gloom. If Maeve were being kept here, Grace reasoned, it was likely to be in one of the upper chambers, where the household's guests—or prisoners—might be secured.

Ascending with deliberate care, she kept one hand on the wooden railing and the other near the pocket of her gown, where she had tucked a small dagger Carew had insisted she carry. Alongside the dagger was a small pistol that Ashley had forced upon her, its weight unfamiliar but oddly reassuring. She prayed she wouldn't need either.

The upper floor was darker still, its windows covered with heavy curtains that stifled even the moonlight. Grace moved from door to door, holding her breath each time she pressed her ear to the wood. Most of the rooms were silent, but she dared not linger long, fearful of being caught lingering.

Finally, she came to a door near the end of the corridor, where a faint sobbing reached her ears. Her heart clenched. It had to be Maeve. Summoning every ounce of courage, Grace turned the handle and slipped inside.

The room was more luxuriously furnished, but the air was thick with despair. The moonlight filtering through a gap in the curtains illuminated the figure on the bed. Maeve lay curled on her side, her hair tangled and her shoulders trembling with suppressed sobs.

"Maeve?" Grace whispered, crossing the room quickly. She knelt beside the bed, her hand gently brushing Maeve's arm. "Maeve, wake up. I am Grace. I have come to help you."

Maeve stirred, her tear-streaked face turning towards her. Her eyes, wide and filled with confusion, turned to Grace's. "Who…?" she began, her voice hoarse.

"Grace Whitford," she said softly. "Your brother sent me. He is outside, waiting to take you home."

Maeve's expression shifted from confusion to disbelief. "Ronan sent you?" she whispered. "How—?"

"There is no time to explain," Grace interrupted. "We must leave before Flynn realizes I am here."

Maeve sat up slowly, wincing as she moved. The faint light revealed dark bruises along her arms and across her cheek. Grace gasped, her stomach twisting with anger and sorrow.

"Maeve," she said, her voice trembling despite her efforts to stay calm, "What has he done to you?"

Maeve's gaze dropped, her hands clutching the blanket as though it might shield her from the shame and fear written across her face. "He said I was being disobedient," she murmured. "That I needed to learn my place."

Grace's anger flared, white-hot and righteous. "You do not belong here," she said firmly. "Flynn is a liar and a coward. You must come with me now."

Maeve hesitated, tears spilling over as she shook her head. "He'll come after us. He said if I tried to leave—he said I'm ruined."

"He will not touch you again," Grace said, her voice fierce. "Ronan is waiting just beyond the gates. He will protect you."

Maeve's eyes searched Grace's face, as though seeking reassurance. Finally, she nodded, her movements slow and tentative. "Very well," she whispered. "I'll go."

Grace squeezed her hand, relief flooding through her. "Get your cloak. The night is cold, but we must hurry."

As Maeve rose from the bed, Grace helped her don a thick cloak around her shoulders. Together, they moved towards the door, their steps silent. The corridors seemed to stretch endlessly before them, each shadow a potential threat.

Finally, they reached the staircase. Maeve hesitated, her grip tightening on Grace's arm. "What shall we do if he's awake and sees us?" she whispered.

"Then we run," Grace replied, her voice firm. "But I will not allow him to stop us."

Maeve nodded, her resolve visibly strengthening. Together, they descended the stairs, the torch near the front door guiding them like a beacon.

The sound of raucous laughter and clinking glasses echoed in the corridor, accompanied by the unmistakable slur of drunken revelry. Grace froze mid-step, her heart pounding so violently she feared it might betray them. They must have gone the wrong way! Beside her, Maeve clutched at her arm, her trembling fingers a silent plea for reassurance. Light spilled from a half-open door ahead. "'Tis him."

A voice rang out in a drunken boast tinged with cruelty. "A toast to our triumph, lads! He thinks he can outwit me? Will he not be surprised to return and find his little sister came to me on her own!"

Another burst of laughter followed, the kind that sent shivers down Grace's spine. She glanced at Maeve, whose wide eyes glistened with barely contained tears. Grace placed a steadying hand on her arm, her whisper barely audible over the din. "We must keep moving. Slowly and as quietly as possible."

Maeve nodded, her breath shallow as they edged closer to the source of the noise. The corridor seemed to stretch endlessly, and Grace feared they would ever reach the end. The smell of ale and sweat was overwhelming as they passed by, and Flynn's laughter felt like a blade poised to strike.

As they slipped past unseen, Grace prayed fervently that the laughter would not suddenly stop, that no shadow would fall across their path. The door was now behind them, but their fear lingered, a suffocating presence urging them onward.

When they reached the threshold, Grace pushed the door open and stepped into the cool night air, pulling Maeve through with her, then shutting it carefully behind her. She prayed their steps were unheard as they hurried back across the drawbridge and towards the waiting shadows where Ronan was hidden.

"Ronan," Grace called softly, her voice carrying just enough to reach him.

He emerged from the darkness, his tall figure silhouetted against the moonlight. His eyes widened as they fell on Maeve, and in an instant, he was at her side, his hands gripping her shoulders as he searched her face.

"Maeve," he breathed, his voice breaking with relief then anger as he saw her beaten face. "What has he done to you?"

She shook her head as though she could not speak of it. "You came for me," she whispered, tears spilling anew.

"*Mo mhuirnín*, I'll always come for you." Ronan pulled her into a fierce embrace, his jaw clenched tightly as he held her. Over her shoulder, his gaze met Grace's, and in that moment, a silent understanding passed between them. She had done what he could not, and for that, she knew he was grateful.

"We must go," Grace reminded them. The night was not over. Flynn would not let Maeve go so easily, and the danger was far from past. Who knew how long they had until they discovered she was gone?

～

"We must gather the others and make haste before he discovers you are missing," Ronan said, making his voice low and urgent as they prepared to depart. The cool night air wrapped around them like a shroud as Ronan tightened his grip on Maeve. He glanced back towards the darkened fortress they had just left, half-expecting Flynn to burst through its heavy doors at any moment. They had to move swiftly before their escape was discovered.

"He drank heavily tonight," she murmured, her tone strangely subdued, as if seeking to explain away the brutality Flynn had inflicted upon her. Ronan's arms tightened around her shoulders. He made no reply to her words—there would be time later to unmask the full depth of Flynn's cruelty and offer what solace and redress he could. For now, escape was paramount. They made their way to a copse of trees where the horses had been hidden.

Maeve was hoisted onto Ronan's gelding, then he helped Grace onto her mount.

"Thank you," he whispered in her ear, the intensity of his voice speaking volumes that words could not capture at present. Later, he would attempt a better way of expressing his gratitude. There was no time for emotion when they were so close to having Maeve safe. What other demons Flynn might have inflicted upon his sister they would deal with in time. What mattered now was that they had recovered her.

He mounted the horse behind Maeve, who was trembling, and tightened his arms around her, though he suspected 'twas fear and nerves more than the cold that caused it.

They moved in near silence, their horses' hooves muffled by the damp earth as they circled to the back of the bailey. The shadows were deep here, offering cover as they approached the grove where Freddy and Joy were to have kept watch.

Joy emerged first, her face lighting up at the sight of Grace. "You have done it!" she whispered, her usual exuberance not tempered by the gravity of the moment.

Together, they made their way around the wall to where Stuart and Patience waited at the servants' entrance. Stuart's eyes widened slightly when he saw Maeve, but he quickly recovered, inclining his head. "Oh, well done, Grace!" Stuart said in quiet approval.

"Yet another case for women in the army, is it not, husband?" Patience said with a wry arch of her brow, though her tone carried relief and pride rather than true jest. It eased the tension in the air, allowing them a moment's respite to acknowledge what Grace had accomplished.

Ashley offered a faint smile. "I shall not argue the point tonight, my dear." He then spoke more gravely to the group: "We must get the ladies to safety."

The group moved quickly, their mounts falling into a tight formation as they rode towards the edge of Flynn's lands. The darkened countryside seemed vast and perilous, the moonlight their only guide. The air was heavy with tension, Ronan reflected, each rider being alert for the first sign of pursuit.

They had nearly reached the safety of the trees when a shout rang out behind them. Ronan twisted in his saddle, his worst fear realized. Flynn and a group of armed men poured through the keep's wall, their torches flaring like malevolent stars in the night. How had they been discovered so quickly?

"Ride!" Ronan commanded, his voice cutting through the chaos. "To the trees!"

The group surged forward, their horses galloping full tilt towards the cover of the forest. The shouts of their pursuers grew louder, the thunder of hooves closing in. Ronan's arms tightened around Maeve, her fear palpable as she clung to him.

Arrows whistled past them, one striking a tree just inches from Grace's head. Ronan's heart clenched as he saw her duck instinctively, her horse surging forward in response to her urgent commands.

They reached the edge of the trees, the dense foliage offering some cover as they weaved between the trunks. The sounds of pursuit grew fainter, but Flynn's men were not easily deterred. Ronan knew they would not stop until they had regained their quarry.

A flash of torchlight upon steel warned Ronan an instant too late. A small knot of Flynn's men had ridden hard around another path and now blocked their escape. Swords and pistols gleamed in the uncertain light. The party skidded to a halt, rearing horses and frantic whinnies adding to the chaos.

Ashley was first to react, drawing his pistol with the practised ease of a military man. He fired a warning shot over the heads of Flynn's brigands. They ducked, startled, but did not retreat.

As they burst into a small clearing, Flynn himself emerged from the shadows, his eyes wild with fury. His horse reared, its hooves striking the air as he levelled a pistol at Ronan.

Ronan dismounted swiftly, easing Maeve from the saddle and

placing her behind the horse for cover. His eyes met Grace's and she followed suit, understanding what he wished her to do, her face pale but resolute. The men advanced slowly, their laughter coarse and their intentions clear.

Flynn dismounted as well, his pistol still aimed. The two men circled each other, the air crackling with tension.

Flynn's eyes glinted with fury and drunken confidence. He brandished a pistol in one hand and a rapier in the other. "Carew!" he shouted drunkenly. "You think to steal what is mine? Give me Maeve, and I might let you slink away with your tail between your legs."

Ronan stepped forward, rigid with contempt. "Maeve is not yours," he said coldly. "She never was!"

"Oh, she is mine, ye need have no doubt!" he taunted, to the sniggering of his men.

Ronan's jaw tightened, barely keeping his fury suppressed. The air was heavy with tension, the only sound that of the horses snorting and stamping. The torches flickered, casting erratic shadows across the faces of Flynn's men, who surrounded him in a loose semicircle, weapons drawn. Their gazes passed between their leader and Ronan.

Ronan drew his sword. It gleamed faintly in the dim light. His voice was cold, cutting through the strain like the blade he held. "Call your men off. This is between you and me."

Flynn tilted his head with mock deliberation, the glint of amusement in his eyes portraying his confidence. "Very well," he drawled, a slow, calculating smile spreading across his face. "En garde," he mocked as he swung his own blade in a circle.

The two men squared off, ready to fight to the death over years of enmity. Ronan adjusted his grip on the hilt, his muscles coiling in preparation. Around them, the onlookers seemed to fade into the periphery. This was not merely a duel; it was a reckoning.

Flynn lunged first, his movements smooth and deliberate, his blade arcing towards Ronan's side. Ronan parried, the clash of steel ringing out sharply. The force of the blow reverberated up his arm, but he countered with a swift thrust aimed at Flynn's chest. Flynn dodged, his grin widening as though he was toying with Ronan.

As the fight progressed, the air filled with the sound of grunts and the scrape of metal. Flynn fought much as Ronan had expected, his strikes wild and ruthless. He moved with the precision of a man who fought often. Yet Ronan, fuelled by fury and the weight of his sister's suffering, matched him blow for blow.

They weaved back and forth, each man testing the other's defences, searching for an opening. Flynn's smile began to falter, replaced by a grim determination as he realized Ronan would not go down easily.

Flynn's blade darted towards Ronan's shoulder, but Ronan parried with a sharp twist of his wrist, creating a resounding clanging of metal. Flynn's smirk twisted into a snarl as he circled like a predator. His eyes glinted with malice, and Ronan felt Flynn's hatred in every move. He returned the feeling in full measure.

In the next instant, Flynn's hand darted to his side, drawing a pistol from beneath his coat. The movement was swift and unmistakable. The click of the hammer being drawn back shattered the pretence of fighting like gentlemen.

Flynn's face was a mask of triumph, his eyes gleaming with dark satisfaction. "This is how it ends, Carew," he sneered. "You lose, and your family pays the price."

Ronan glared at him, his jaw set, defiance raging within despite his disadvantage. "I've come to expect nothing less than dishonour from you," he said hoarsely.

Flynn's lips curled and his finger tightened on the pistol's trigger, and for an agonizing moment, time seemed to stand still. He should never have trusted Flynn to fight like a gentleman, and all he could think about was dying in front of Maeve and Grace.

"No!" Maeve's scream tore through the night, raw and filled with terror.

And then, before Ronan could react, shots split the air—sharp, deafening cracks. Flynn's body jerked violently, the force of the bullet driving him back. His pistol fired into the sky, wild and missing its target. For a moment, Flynn stood frozen, his eyes wide with shock, before he crumpled to the ground.

Ronan numbly turned and saw Grace standing a short distance away. She held a pistol in her trembling hands, the barrel still smoking. Her face was pale, her expression one of shock.

Then he saw Stuart to the side, who gave a little shake of his head, and Ronan was grateful for his action, the calm precision of a soldier. His pistol remained raised for a heartbeat longer before he lowered it, his steady gaze fixed on the fallen rogue.

Flynn's men, who had watched the duel with bated breath, now hesitated, their confidence shaken by the sight of their leader's lifeless body. One by one, they lowered their weapons and began to back away, retreating into the darkness.

Maeve let out a sob as the dam finally broke. Joy and Patience rushed forward, their relief palpable as they surrounded the group, checking for injuries and murmuring words of reassurance.

Ronan strode to Grace, his gaze intense. She still held the pistol, her knuckles white against the dark metal, as though she could not let it go. Gently, he reached out and covered her hands with his own and eased the weapon from her grip.

"Grace," he said quietly, his voice thick with a mixture of awe and gratitude.

Grace blinked, as though coming out of a trance. "He was going to kill you," she whispered.

Her words hung in the air, a simple truth that shook Ronan to his core. He placed the pistol on the ground and stepped closer, his hands resting lightly on her shoulders. Then he gathered her into his arms.

Ronan held her tightly, memorizing how she felt in his arms. She melted into the embrace, her cheek resting against his chest. He owed her more than he could ever express, more than he could fathom in this moment. Flynn was dead, and his family was safe—for now. It was Grace who had stepped into the fray when all seemed lost by helping Maeve escape.

Grace's breath hitched, and she shook her head slightly. "I missed," she said, her tone hollow.

"You would have done it," he murmured, his voice low and filled with wonder. "You would have killed for me."

Her eyes glistened with unshed tears, but she said nothing, merely nodding as though unsure how to respond.

Together, they gathered Maeve and the others, turning their backs on the battlefield and leading their horses towards the road that took them away. The night felt lighter, the immediate threat of Flynn gone for now. And though this was far from over, Ronan allowed himself to hope for peace.

CHAPTER 15

The ride back to Donnellan Castle was shrouded in unreality, Grace faintly registering the rhythmic beat of hooves upon the earth. The mood was sombre, the events of the night hanging heavily over them. The mist that had clung to the ground earlier had thickened to fog, its damp embrace lending an oppressive chill to the journey. Grace rode near the centre of the party, her shaking hands tight upon the reins, her thoughts like a swirling snowstorm she could not seem to see through.

She had tried to shoot a man.

Her fingers flexed without her consciously making them do so, as if they could still feel the weight of the pistol, the cold metal against her skin. The memory of that moment was seared into her mind: the glint of Flynn's pistol, the sneering triumph on his face, the raw panic that had seized her chest as he aimed at Ronan. She had acted without thinking, moved by some primal instinct she had not known she possessed. And though her shot had missed its mark—thank heavens Ashley's had not—she could not escape the knowledge that she had been perfectly willing to kill for him.

The numbness she felt was not from the cold but from the enormity of what she had done, or nearly done. She was not a soldier, not a hero in one of her stories. She was Grace Whitford, the quiet sister, the one who preferred books to ballrooms, who never sought to stand out. And yet, tonight, she had lifted a weapon and tried to end a man's life.

She would do it again. It was not a feeling she welcomed, but it was there all the same, a steely thread running through the fabric of her shock. It had been necessary, she told herself. It'd had to be done.

The thought churned in her mind as the miles passed. Flynn had been a monster and deserved his punishment. The marks on Maeve's face, the fear in her eyes, spoke volumes of his cruelty. He had sought to kill Carew, and Grace had been compelled to stop him. She was grateful—deeply, fervently grateful—that Ashley's shot had ended it instead, sparing her the weight of having to bear Flynn's death upon her own conscience. Not that it was easy for Ashley, but he'd had experience of such things in the war.

As they rode on, her gaze drifted to Patience, who rode confidently beside her husband. Patience, who had killed a man to save Ashley's life and seemed none the worse for it. Grace had not asked her sister about that moment before, but now she wondered. Did Patience feel this same strange numbness? Did she lie awake at night, replaying the scene in her mind? Or had she simply accepted it as part of life's cruel necessities and dismissed it with her customary strength?

"Are you cold?" Patience's voice broke through her reverie, and Grace started slightly, realizing that her sister was watching her with quiet concern.

"A little," Grace admitted, though she had not noticed. She offered a faint smile to reassure her. "I am well enough."

Patience regarded her for a moment longer, then nodded. "If you need to rest, say so. We will stop."

Grace shook her head. "The sooner we are back, the better."

Patience nodded her understanding, glancing back at Maeve, who rode behind Ronan on his gelding. She was slumped against her brother, her exhaustion and trauma evident in every line of her body. Patience's gaze softened. "We did right to come along."

The conversation lapsed, and the party rode on, the looming outline of Donnellan Castle growing closer with every passing mile. The journey felt endless, but Grace welcomed the monotony of it. It gave her time to sort through her thoughts, to try to make sense of the whirlwind of emotions churning within her.

When at last they reached the gates of the castle, the sky was almost light. The household anxiously awaited their arrival, and servants hurried to meet them, their faces pale with worry. Ronan dismounted first, carefully helping Maeve from the saddle. She clung to him, her steps unsteady as he guided her inside.

Grace slid from her own mount, her legs stiff from the ride. Patience was at her side in an instant, steadying her with a firm hand. "Come," she said gently. "You need rest."

Rest. It sounded so simple, so natural, and yet Grace doubted she would find it easily. Still, she allowed herself to be led inside, the familiar warmth of the castle wrapping around her like a protective cloak.

The group dispersed quickly. Ashley directed the servants to see to the horses, while Carew and Lady Donnellan escorted Maeve to her chambers. Patience, Freddy, and Joy were shown to their chambers, all ready for their beds. Grace followed, her steps slow and deliberate, as though each one carried the weight of the night's events, but she was not ready to sleep.

Once in the sitting room, she found Theo curled in the chair, and Grace scooped him up and held on to him for solace. She sank into a chair by the fire, the warmth seeping into her chilled bones. She took comfort in watching the crackle of the flames and the soothing purrs emanating from Theo's tiny body.

"You were very brave," Carew said, interrupting her mind's wanderings. He leaned against the door frame, his face shadowed with exhaustion but his eyes warm as they met hers.

Grace glanced at him, startled by his presence. "I do not feel brave," she admitted. "I acted without thinking." *I would have done anything to save you*, she thought but did not add.

"You saw what needed to be done, and you did it."

Grace shook her head, her brow furrowing. "It does not feel that way. I...I am not sure how I feel. Grateful that Ashley intervened, I think...and yet, if he had not..." She trailed off, unable to finish the thought.

Carew had somehow moved forward and was kneeling before her. He placed a hand on Grace's. "You did what you could to protect Maeve and I. That's what matters."

Grace nodded slowly, though her mind still wrestled with the enormity of it all. She thought again of Patience, of her sister's unwavering composure despite her own history with violence. Perhaps she could imitate her sister; find a way to find peace amid the turmoil. Or perhaps it simply took time.

"How is Maeve?"

"Maeve is resting," he said quietly. "She asked after you. She said you saved us both."

Grace's cheeks flushed, and she looked down at her hands. "I did not—"

"You did," Ronan interrupted gently, his tone leaving no room for argument. "What you did tonight took courage, Grace. I owe you more than I can say."

Her throat tightened, and she managed a small nod. "I am only glad it is over," she murmured, "and that she is safe."

"As am I," Ronan said, his gaze lingering on her for a moment before he stood up and stepped back. "You should rest. We all should."

He extended his hand, and Grace rose, her movements slow and deliberate as the heaviness of the night pressed down upon her once more. She accepted his hand, the warmth of his touch steadying her for a fleeting moment. When she stood, her eyes met his briefly, and in them, she saw not the resolute Lord Carew but the man beneath—the brother who had fought so fiercely for his sister, the man who had fought Kilroy for her.

"Goodnight, my lord," she said softly, her voice carrying the weight of her exhaustion but also something else, something unspoken.

Ronan hesitated, his hand lingering against hers for just a moment longer. Then, as if compelled by something beyond himself, he gently drew her into an embrace. It was not the embrace of triumph or relief but one of gratitude and understanding. His arms encircled her carefully, almost reverently, as though he feared she might shatter under the weight of all they had endured. And also to avoid squishing the cat.

"Goodnight, Grace," he murmured close to her ear, his voice soft and steady.

For a moment, she allowed herself to rest there, the faint scent of the sea lingering on his coat and the warmth of his presence offering a fragile comfort. She felt the strength in his arms, not just the physical strength that had carried him through the night but the quiet fortitude that had brought them all to safety. And yet, she sensed the weariness within him, as if he perhaps still carried some burden.

When they parted, her cheeks were warm, though she told herself it was from the firelight. She nodded once more, her fingers brushing against the folds of her skirt as she stepped back. "Goodnight, Ronan," she repeated, this time without formality, the name slipping past her lips with a familiarity she had not intended.

However, her mind refused to find ease. What would happen tomorrow—or the day after? She dreaded the thought of leaving him. There was a finality in it that made her chest tighten, though she could not fully explain why. She had not come to Donnellan by design, but she had certainly become a different person from the one who had left England. She had acted with courage, faced danger, and stood firm when it mattered most. All because of him.

The idea of departing, of returning to a life where their paths would seldom cross again, filled her with a quiet dread. She had known him in moments of both strength and vulnerability, seen the depths of his character, and found something she had not realized she had been seeking. Could she simply walk away from that? It seemed she had little choice. Whilst there had been some closeness, and friendship, there had been no hints of anything more.

Surprisingly, when she undressed and slipped beneath the heavy blankets, sleep came. The day's events, the fear and resolve, the unspoken emotions all seemed to catch up with her at once, pulling her into the oblivion of sleep.

～

Ronan stood at the window of his study, the early morning light casting long shadows across the room. The fire in the hearth had burned low, the embers glowing faintly. He should also seek his bed, but his thoughts were too heavy and all-consuming to permit any comfort from sleep. He stared out over the rolling hills beyond Donnellan, their rugged beauty softened by the pale mist that lingered over the land.

Flynn was dead.

The knowledge should have brought him satisfaction, perhaps even relief, but instead, it left him hollow. The fury that had driven him to this point seemed now to dissipate, leaving in its place a gnawing emptiness. Flynn's death would not undo the harm he had wrought. It would not erase the marks left upon Maeve's body, nor the scars upon her spirit. And it certainly had not ended the old wounds of the feud between their families.

Lord Corlach would want retribution. Flynn might have been a scoundrel and a manipulator, but he had been Corlach's son, and his death would not be ignored. The feud was not over—it had merely shifted its shape. Flynn had been one enemy among many, a symbol of the larger conflict that had plagued their families for generations. And now the animosity would only deepen.

Ronan's gaze drifted to the fields below, thinking of where Maeve had used to play as a child. He had failed to protect his sister, failed to shield her from Flynn's machinations. That failure weighed heavily on him now, a constant reminder of the cost of generations of pride and the lingering consequences of the feud. Maeve was safe, yes, but she was not whole. The light in her eyes had dimmed, and Ronan did not know if it would ever return.

A soft knock at the door pulled him from his thoughts. He turned as the door opened, and his mother entered, her presence as steady and quiet as ever. She hesitated for a moment, her worried gaze casting over him before she stepped into the room.

"You do not sleep," she said softly, her voice softly scolding. "The household is concerned."

Ronan turned back to the window, his jaw tightening. "It changes nothing."

His mother closed the door behind her, her footsteps light as she crossed the room. "When will you tell me what happened?" she asked, gently probing. "Your father asks after you. I had to tell him about Maeve when you left again without greeting him earlier. Word reached him before I had a chance to warn his valet."

He sighed heavily. "I will see him forthwith. Perhaps it is best if we go together and I tell you both."

"First, this just came by messenger for you."

The familiar crest pressed into the wax caught Ronan's attention immediately. It was the crest of Corlach. He took the letter from her with a furrowed brow and broke the seal, his fingers steady despite the weight he felt pressing on him. The parchment was crisp, the handwriting bold and deliberate. He read it in silence, his emotions shifting from guarded curiosity to contemplative.

DEAR LORD CAREW,

WORD *of my son's death has reached me. Though my son's actions brought about his own end, I cannot deny the role our feud has played in perpetuating such reckless enmity. For all our families have lost over the years, I have come to see the folly in carrying this bitterness further.*

I beg you—let this end here and now. Flynn is gone, and with him, let there be no more grievances between us. Let there be no further bloodshed, no more families torn asunder by hatred borne of wounds long scarred over. I am an old man and do not wish my legacy to be hatred.

I pray Lady Maeve is unharmed. Whatever Flynn's sins, I grieve if they caused her pain.

CORLACH

RONAN FOLDED THE LETTER SLOWLY, his mind turning over each word. Corlach's tone was not one of defiance but of regret, a rare sentiment from a man who had been his family's adversary for so many years. For the first time, Ronan felt the stirrings of a possibility he had scarcely dared to consider: peace.

"Bad news?" His mother's voice broke through his thoughts, and he looked up to find her watching him with quiet concern.

"No," he replied, his tone carefully measured, "not bad but unexpected. Corlach writes to propose an end to the feud."

Her brows lifted in surprise. "Truly?"

Ronan nodded, his gaze distant. "He admits Flynn's responsibility in all of this and asks that we let it end here. He claims to grieve for Maeve's suffering." His voice hardened slightly on the last words, the thought of Flynn's treatment of his sister still raw in his mind.

She stepped closer, her hand brushing his arm. "Perhaps he means it," she said gently. "You need not trust him to accept peace. This will be a relief to your father. His own culpability weighs heavily on him."

Ronan nodded and together they made their way to speak with him.

The door to his father's chambers opened slowly, the familiar scent of wood smoke wafting out to greet him. Lord Donnellan sat in his usual chair near the hearth, his once-imposing frame now frail with age and illness. Despite his weakened state, his eyes were sharp as they met Ronan's.

"You have news," his father said, his voice gravelly but steady. It was not a question.

"I do," Ronan replied, stepping inside and motioning for his mother to follow. She hesitated briefly but complied, her presence a quiet support that Ronan found himself grateful for.

Ronan held up the folded letter. "A message from Corlach," he said. "He proposes we end the feud. Flynn is dead, and he wishes to let the feud die along with him."

The elder man's brows furrowed, his gaze narrowing. "And you believe him?"

"I believe he is weary of this fight, as are we all," Ronan replied. "Flynn's death, though just, has left a heavy mark. To carry on this feud would only deepen the wounds he has left behind."

"It has never lessened enmity before." His father leaned back in his chair, his expression inscrutable. "And what of Maeve?" he asked after a moment. "How fares my daughter?"

Ronan's jaw tightened when he thought of what Flynn had done to her. "She is safe now," he answered quietly, "but the wounds Flynn inflicted cannot be mended with kind words and assurances. I failed her, Father."

"Maeve does not see you as a failure. She sees you as her brother, the man who risked everything to save her. That matters, whether you believe it or not." His mother's voice was firm but kind.

"The blame is mine. I should have ended this long ago," his father interjected.

Ronan's chest tightened at their words, but he nodded slowly.

"She will heal in time. All we can do is love her and give her time to find her strength again."

Lord Donnellan's sharp gaze did not waver as he considered. Though his body had grown frail, the steel of his mind remained unbroken. Ronan's father studied his son for a long moment before speaking. "If Corlach truly seeks peace, it would be folly to refuse him. Both families have endured enough. I will pen a reply."

The decision settled over the room like a quiet benediction. Ronan felt the tension in his shoulders ease slightly, though he knew the road ahead would still be fraught with challenges.

"Who are these guests your mother mentioned? And what is this I hear about a young lady travelling with you?"

Ronan stiffened slightly but recovered quickly. "Miss Grace Whitford," he said, his tone steady. "She accompanied me here under extraordinary circumstances through no fault of her own. She is the sister of Lady Westwood, Lady Rotham, and Mrs. Ashley Stuart, all of whose husbands you are acquainted with. The guests are her family come after her. We owe all of them—especially her—a debt of gratitude."

Lord Donnellan's brows lifted slightly, a flicker of interest passing over his face. "Indeed?"

Ronan hesitated, then began, his voice quiet but firm. "She risked herself to save Maeve. She entered Flynn's home under the guise of seeking shelter, gaining access where I could not. She found Maeve and brought her out to safety, despite the great risk to herself. And when Flynn came after us and threatened me, she did not falter." He did not mask his pride. "Her courage is remarkable."

His mother, beside her husband, observed Ronan closely, a faint smile playing on her lips.

He glanced at her, a flicker of discomfort contorting his features, though he did not deny her the assumptions she was no doubt making. "She deserves the highest praise for what she has done. Without her, we might not have succeeded."

Lord Donnellan leaned back in his chair, his hands resting on the arms. "A lady of such character should be acknowledged. I should like to meet her, Ronan. It seems I owe her my thanks."

Ronan inclined his head. "I will arrange it, Father. But for now, you must rest."

His father waved a hand dismissively. "Do not coddle me, boy. I am frail, but I am not feeble. Go and see that this young woman is properly received."

"Yes, Father."

As he left the room, Ronan's mind churned with conflicting emotions. He had spoken of Grace with truth, but in doing so, he had revealed more of his own thoughts than he had intended. Her presence with him last night had shifted something within him, though he could not yet name what that was.

As he walked through the quiet halls of his home, Ronan felt a glimmer of hope take root that the ghosts of the past might finally find peace. Perhaps the feud truly could end here, and with it, the cycle of pain that had defined so much of his heritage. And perhaps, just perhaps, the future held something brighter—something worth fighting for in a different way.

CHAPTER 16

When Grace awoke, daylight was filtering through the heavy curtains of her chambers, casting faint shadows across the carpet. For a moment, she lay wrapped in the warmth of the bed, but unwelcome thoughts began to intrude and, lest she give in to their power, she decided to rise and take a walk. She did not feel ready to face anyone—not yet. Something about the outdoors beckoned to her, a silent call from the cliffs she had glimpsed the day before.

With quiet determination, Grace dressed in a simple gown from her sister, and wrapped herself in a heavy cloak against the morning chill. Most of the household still slept, no doubt exhausted from their harrowing night and the emotions that had accompanied it. The silence gave her a sense of solitude, a small reprieve from facing others just yet.

As she made her way through the castle, her eyes drifted over the interior steeped in an ancient grandeur that spoke of its long and storied past. She passed through the great hall, which was flanked by roaring fires at either end to ward off the autumn draughts. The towering beams overhead, darkened with age, seemed to bow with the weight of centuries, and the tapestries along the walls hung still, reminding her of a similar scene the night before. She walked on, determined to move past the memory.

Now in the grey light of morning, she could see the outlines of crenellated towers and weathered walls. The very stones seemed alive with history, whispering tales of long-past battles and enduring resilience. She could almost imagine archers standing guard upon the walls, their arrows poised to repel marauding knights.

She moved towards the stone wall that bordered the courtyard, drawn by the rhythmic waves against the rocks below. She watched, mesmerized by the sight, as though the sea might provide answers or insight into her future. The waves surged and broke against the cliffs, sending sprays of white foam into the air before retreating once more.

What happens next? The question was omnipresent, because Grace did not feel at all like the same person who had left England just over a week ago.

How could she return to her old life as though nothing had changed? The events of the past days had stirred something within her. Strength, resolve, longing…but also unease. How could she return to the life she had left behind, to the quiet parlours and the staid expectations of Society? Three of her sisters were now married, their futures secured, and she was expected to follow the same path. Yet the thought filled her with a quiet dread. How could she be content again, knowing what she did now? Knowing how much more of life there was to be had?

She could no more transform herself into someone she was not than she could stop the tide that came in below. She would never be the loud, confident woman who charmed a room effortlessly. She was quiet and reflective, but she was also more than that. This journey had shown her a side of herself she had not known existed—courage she had never thought herself capable of, strength she had not believed she possessed.

If it had not been for the strange twist of fate that had left her on Lord Carew's ship, she might never have known this feeling—that of leaving, of stepping into something greater than the small world she had once inhabited.

For that, she ought to be grateful. And once her heart healed, perhaps she would be. Would Carew feel obligated to offer for her? The thought sent a pang through her chest. She didn't think she could bear it. To be tied for life out of duty was a heavy burden to bear, both for the one who gave and the one who received. Yet she could not deny the spark of hope that flickered within her. Could there be more between them? Could he, in time, come to feel for her what she could not deny she already felt for him?

Grace knew he cared for her now—his actions had shown as much. He had shown her kindness, even tenderness, but was that enough? Was it any more than he would show a beloved sister? She shook her head, almost laughing bitterly at her own musings. She was no siren to tempt him into wild confessions of unending devotion. Grace knew herself too well to entertain such notions. Still, the question lingered: what came next? Would they simply leave this place, parting as though the events they had shared were merely like a storm passing in the night?

The injustice of it all formed a tight knot in her chest. She had so little control over her future, so little power to shape her own path. It made her want to scream, to rail against the constraints placed upon her by circumstance and Society. Instead, she closed her eyes, the sound of the sea filling her ears as she tried to quiet her thoughts.

"Grace! There you are!" A familiar voice broke through her reflections, and she turned to see Patience approaching, her cheeks pink from exertion. "I have been searching everywhere for you."

Grace offered a small smile, though her expression betrayed her weariness. "You have found me," she said simply.

Patience came to stand beside her, leaning against the wall and following Grace's gaze out to the sea. "You have changed, Grace," she said after a moment, her tone contemplative, and her gaze all-seeing. "Since you left."

Grace turned back to the sea, her hands clasping the edge of her cloak. "I feel changed," she admitted. "I feel…unsettled. It is as though I no longer know who I am."

"Perhaps that is because you're becoming who you are meant to be," Patience suggested, her voice thoughtful. "Change is rarely comfortable, but that does not mean it isn't right."

Grace hesitated, her heart thudding as she considered whether to speak the truth that had been weighing on her. "Patience," she began tentatively, "supposing I feel something—for someone—that I cannot imagine being returned?"

Patience turned to her, her expression suddenly intent. "You speak of Carew."

Grace's cheeks flushed, but she nodded. "There is much more to him than he lets people see. He is kind, and brave, and more than I could ever have imagined. Yet I cannot think he could feel the same for me...and the thought of him offering out of obligation..." Her voice faltered.

Patience placed a hand on Grace's arm, her touch steady and reassuring. "You are more than you believe yourself to be, Grace, and I think he sees that. Whether his feelings are what you hope, I cannot say, but I do not think him the kind of man to offer out of obligation."

Grace looked down, the waves crashing far below echoing the turmoil within her. "I do not know what I should do," she confessed. "I feel as though I am standing on the edge of something, but I cannot see where it leads."

Patience smiled gently. "Sometimes the best thing you can do is take the next step, whatever that may be, however uncomfortable, and trust yourself to find the way."

Grace nodded slowly, her sister's words settling over her like the first rays of sunlight breaking through the mist. Perhaps she did not need to have all the answers now. Perhaps it was enough to simply take that first step.

"But in order to do that, I need to be here, not returning to England," she felt compelled to point out.

Patience laughed. "'Twould be more difficult in this situation, I grant you. Perhaps we can stay a few more days, if invited. I will speak to Ashley, and he can send word to Westwood that you are found and well. Are you coming back inside?"

"Not just yet."

Patience kissed her on the cheek and then left her.

Grace decided to explore a bit more—there was a whole other side to the estate where the renowned Donnellan horses were no doubt pastured. She'd rather Carew show them to her but she was not ready to go inside. As luck would have it, she ran into Paddy. She had quite forgotten he went from cabin boy to stable boy when on land.

He stopped and made her an awkward bow.

"How is Theo, miss? I would 'ave come to visit, but we aren't really allowed in the 'ouse except on special occasions."

"Well, then I shall bring Theo to you. I am certain he would enjoy the stables and his sister Evelina is here now as well. Two of my sisters have come to visit me here and have brought one of the other kittens."

"I got sisters, too," he said sympathetically, which made her laugh.

"I will inform the maid who has been caring for the kittens that you have special permission to help with them."

"Cor, would you, miss? I'll even share one with Barry."

"See that you do. That would be an excellent thing."

He hurried back to his duties and she watched him go with a smile.

∽

AFTER LEAVING his father's room, Ronan paused at one of the landings and looked out of the window when a movement caught his eye. There Grace stood, overlooking the cliffs, a beam of sunlight breaking through the clouds as if its entire purpose was to shine right on her. Ronan did not need the heavens to point out her angelic qualities. He knew them very well by now, which is why he still hesitated to offer someone like himself to her. He wasn't quite the devil, but neither was he the honourable man she deserved.

He moved closer to the window, as if drawn to her light, and saw that she was, in fact, conversing with her sister, Patience. Indeed, they were deep in conversation, Patience was as animated as ever, her hands gesturing expressively, while Grace listened with her customary quiet, thoughtful air. The faintest smile played on Grace's lips, and Ronan found himself lingering over that sight, remembering the feel of her kiss on his lips.

Her family had come to save her from him and scandal, and it was likely they had succeeded. Why then was he now so resentful about it when he should feel relief? Instead, he wanted to be with her without the strain he'd felt about Flynn and Maeve.

'Twas likely they were already preparing to depart, which also led him close to despair. He needed more time to be able to sort through his feelings and hers. With Flynn no longer being a threat, he felt more free to do so, but he also wanted to have time to determine Grace's own feelings. Was it better to let her go and then return to London after she'd had time away from him to reflect?

Certainly, without fear of ruin or scandal, that would be the honourable thing to do, but now that he'd seen the real Grace Whitford, he was selfishly reluctant to let her go.

Somehow, subconsciously, he had begun moving to where she was, drawn to her. By the time he reached the terrace wall, he barely caught sight of her heading towards the stables. Then he saw Paddy and understood why she'd gone there. Paddy was already turning away by the time Ronan reached her.

Grace turned when she heard him. "My lord! I had not realized you were there."

"I have just arrived. How are you this morning?" He searched her face for signs of distress. Only a shade of dark purple beneath her eyes hinted that perhaps she had not slept as well as she ought. Doubtless his own reflected something similar as he'd yet to seek his bed.

"I am well, thank you, although I did not sleep for long," she confessed as though she'd guessed his thoughts. "How is your sister?"

"I believe she is still sleeping. My mother gave her a draught."

Grace nodded as though that was just what should have happened. "Would you care to walk a little?"

Her eyes twinkled. "I had thought to look at your famed stables, sir, but upon seeing Paddy, I was reminded your sailors were also some of your stable workers and might not care to see me."

"They've no fear of the sea goddess here." He tried to hold back a smile and failed. "There will be some horses in the paddock," he suggested and held out his arm to her.

She took it a bit hesitantly, as if she, too, were not certain what came next.

It had been a while since he had led her in such a formal manner. In fact, it was when they had presented themselves as very different people, two Seasons ago. He found that he very much disliked being formal with her at all. He'd not been himself for some time and not at all like he'd been before Flynn had begun threatening his family. When he thought how very little time he had now to convince her he could be worthy, his chest thumped hard with what must be panic.

Should he speak with Stuart and Patience and convince them to stay a few days? It was what his father—and very likely his mother too—wanted, he thought wryly. Ronan wanted to make sure it was also what he and Grace wanted.

"This is what the rest of Ireland looks like," he said inadequately, as they stood before a lush green meadow tucked into a valley surrounded by rolling hills.

The pretty silver mare she'd ridden the night before pranced over, demanding attention, and Ronan watched as Grace stroked her soothingly.

"You seem troubled," Grace said gently, drawing him back to the present. "Is something wrong?"

Ronan glanced at her, startled by her perceptiveness, but quickly recovered. "Not troubled," he said after a beat, though he realized how unconvincing it sounded. "Merely…reflective."

Grace tilted her head, her eyes narrowing in mild amusement. "I would not have taken you for the brooding sort, Lord Carew."

"Nor I, but it appears you bring out the worst in me," he said, his voice frank, but not unkind.

Grace blinked, caught off guard, as though he'd slapped her. "If that is the case, then perhaps I ought to leave you to seethe in peace."

Ronan stepped forward before he could think better of it. "On the contrary," he said, his tone deepening. "You have proven far too adept at unsettling me for me to wish you gone."

Grace looked at a loss for words. "Unsettling you is a...desired quality?"

The moment hung between them, like a butterfly hovering, uncertain where to land. Ronan could scarcely believe the words had left his mouth, and a flicker of nervousness crept in—*nervousness,* of all things. It was both absurd and undeniable. "I rather think it is."

Her cheeks coloured faintly, and she turned back to the mare as though the horse's mane demanded her full attention.

Clearing his throat, he turned the conversation to safer ground. "My father has expressed a desire to meet you," he said, his tone returning to something more familiar. "He wishes to thank you properly for what you have done."

Grace smiled. "That is unnecessary, but I would be honoured to meet him before we leave."

Ronan nodded, his mind already leaping ahead. "Perhaps I might speak with Major Stuart and Patience. There is no need for such haste in your departure. My parents would appreciate the company, and the castle has been far too quiet of late."

Grace looked at him for a long moment, as though searching his face for something unspoken. "Only your parents would appreciate the company, my lord?" she asked softly, yet rather boldly.

Ronan's lips twisted into the faintest of smiles. "I would as well," he admitted.

"I should very much like to stay longer and see more of Ireland, and...appreciate the company."

Ronan did not hold back a wide smile. "My father wants to host a large gathering to celebrate, which is something indeed since he rarely leaves his chambers to dine these days. We often join him for meals in his sitting room. So you see, you are doing all of us a favour."

He could see she was not convinced.

"I do not wish to be fussed over. Ashley was the one who actually disposed of Flynn."

"But you were the one who rescued Maeve, Grace." Then he tenderly tucked some stray hair that had escaped her bonnet behind her ear. Her breathing hitched, making his heart rejoice even though he knew he should stop tempting himself.

Her cheeks blushed a charming pink, and the devil in him could not resist a taste of the forbidden fruit. He leaned down and sampled her lips, and there was no doubt it was anything brotherly this time.

Hesitant at first, she learned quickly and kissed him back, winding her arms about his neck. He had to convince himself to step away.

Her expression was distraught.

"Lass, I should not be kissing you."

"Why not? I am hardly protesting."

"And you should be. You will not be forced to wed me now, thanks to your family."

She looked as though he'd slapped her and his heart clenched, yet he knew it was best to say it. "You deserve much better than me, Grace. You would regret the day ere long."

"Because of your past."

"Aye, because I have done things that would shame you."

"I see. And in your future? No, pay me no mind." She looked down and shook her head. "You should not be made to pay for my dreadful mistake. But please, if you do not want me for your wife, at least have the decency to say so. I know I am not dashing and beautiful like those ladies with whom you are accustomed."

"Grace, 'tis not that at all. You can have any man you want." He pleaded with her to understand he was doing this for her own good.

"Then you are just a coward, my lord," she said, then turned and hurried away. Ronan did not chase after her because she was right—which confirmed she deserved better than him.

CHAPTER 17

Grace wanted to be rational, but she was devastated. She had not even been able to savour her beautiful first real kiss, for he had then ruined it for her—and just when she had begun to hope he might offer for her, and not even completely out of duty. Yet he would spare her that indignity, apparently. What kind of man was he? She must not really know him at all. She had been lured into thinking their shared experience somehow bound them together in a special way.

That hope had vanished within seconds and a few cold words.

She was silly to have hoped. A man like him would not want to be settled for life with a shy mouse like her.

All she wanted to do was retreat to her room and wallow in self-pity, but even she would not be allowed that today. Lady Maeve was standing outside Grace's door as if she'd been seeking her. But Grace was tender-hearted and her woes were nothing to what Lady Maeve had suffered. She still bore deep, dark bruises on her face and a swollen, cut lip.

"Good morning, Miss Whitford. You have already been out this morning?"

"Please, call me Grace. I have been on a walk, and am lost in admiration for your beautiful home."

"Thank you. Would you join me in my sitting room for some chocolate?"

"Of course. Let me put down my bonnet and pelisse." She laid those on a chest in her room and then followed the girl down the carpeted hall to a lovely set of chambers furnished in pomona green and cream. There was already a tray with chocolate and rolls awaiting them.

They sat down and Maeve poured out the steaming beverage for her. "Thank you," Grace said, accepting the cup and saucer. She sensed that Lady Maeve had something to say, so she waited for her to speak.

"I did not have the chance to thank you for what you did last night to help me," she began. "I realize I put a great many people in danger. It was never my intention to hurt anyone—in fact, I thought it would make everything better."

Grace reached out and took Maeve's hand; it was trembling while her other one wiped away tears that spilled over from her large, sapphire eyes.

"Now Flynn is dead because of me." She lowered her head to compose herself.

Grace could see that Maeve was grieving for the man even though he did not deserve those feelings. *Sometimes, it seems a heart loves despite what is best for it*, she thought. Love truly did not seem to have a direct line of reasoning with the mind—as Grace's own heart could currently attest to.

"You are safe now and no one blames you." Grace fervently hoped the girl's parents had not said otherwise, but she did not think she had misjudged them. They seemed relieved she was home and safe.

"How can they not? Ronan tried to warn me. How could he forgive that?"

"They know you were manipulated and they love you more than anything. Your brother knows you were not being spiteful."

"I don't know if I will ever be able to forgive myself for being such a fool."

Grace could sympathize completely with that notion.

"Mother says I was only infatuated and my heart will heal in time. I will never be so reckless as to love again. Who would even want me now?"

"Anyone would be a fool not to want you, my lady."

"You are very kind to say so, but it is not as though this can be hushed up."

Grace felt bile in her mouth at those words. How conveniently her own situation was to be erased as though it had never happened. She was to pretend they'd merely gone on a little visit to Ireland, when her whole world had been overturned. Perhaps she should be grateful, but she was devastated.

"Are you going to marry my brother?" the girl asked, clearly oblivious to what had just occurred between Grace and Carew. Grace had been distracted in her introspections, and Maeve's words shocked her.

"I-I..." Why did Grace hesitate to answer truthfully? Because it would make it more real?

"I have always wished for a sister," Maeve continued, again oblivious to the discomfort the words inflicted.

"I do not think she will be me, though I should be delighted to call you such."

"But I just saw you outside."

Grace gasped. "I am sorry you saw that. He does not intend that we should wed, however."

"How dare he treat you in such a manner! And he was lecturing me!" Maeve's sadness quickly turned to fury.

"Please, my lady, do not be angry with him. It is my fault entirely, and it was an accident that placed me aboard his ship. I would no more wish for him to be shackled to someone he did not wish for than for you to be estranged from your family."

"It certainly looked as though he was participating well enough," Maeve argued.

Grace reached out and put a hand on Lady Maeve's arm. "Please," she pleaded. "It was a mistake. Would you want someone forced to marry you when they did not wish it?"

"No, of course not. I just do not understand his behaviour."

Nor did Grace, but she did not wish to dwell on it any longer. In fact, she would beg Patience and Ashley to leave on the morrow. Being forced to see Carew and pretend she was not heartbroken was about the worst thing she could imagine at this moment.

The girl let out a heavy sigh. "I suppose you will be leaving soon, then."

"Yes."

"How I envy that you can leave. There is nothing for me here, and I will be shunned unless I marry quickly."

Sadly, Grace knew that to be true. It was the way of their world.

"You have parents who love you. I envy you that." She would give anything to have her parents back.

"Oh! Forgive me. I did not mean…"

"You could not know," Grace reassured her. "They have been gone a long time now, and my sisters love me well. I am certain I would feel the need to escape were I in your shoes. In fact, perhaps something might be arranged whereby you can come to England with us for a while."

Her face lit up at the prospect. "Oh, do you think so?"

"My sister, Joy, will be entering Society, and I know she would welcome the company. I realize you were unable to meet her last night, but she has come with us. Shall I ring for her and you may become acquainted?"

"I would like that very much. I confess I did not notice the others with us, only that there were others present."

Grace pulled on the bell-rope to ring for a servant.

"My sister, Patience, and her husband, Major Stuart, as well as our dear friend, Mr. Cunningham, were also in the party."

"To think so many strangers were willing to help me. You knew me not at all, yet you willingly risked your life to help me."

"As to the first, your brother is not a stranger at all. It is Major Stuart's position in the army to do such things, and your brother has helped my family a time or two in dangerous situations. We were all very willing to help."

A maid entered and Grace conveyed the request to send Joy to them.

Joy must have been nearby, for she appeared quickly with both kittens in tow. She smiled at Maeve. "Good morning, Grace. I was just on my way to take the kittens outside."

"Make your curtsy to Lady Maeve first, please, since we had no opportunity to do so last night. Lady Maeve, this is my sister, Joy."

Lady Maeve stood and returned the curtsy. "It is a pleasure, Miss Joy. May I see one of the kittens?"

Nothing delighted Joy more than someone who shared her love of animals. She plucked Evalina from her especially sewn pouch and handed the kitten over. Grace saw Theo's head spring up next, and she couldn't resist taking him for herself. She'd missed his cuddles last night. He seemed to have missed her in turn, as his loud purrs reverberated as soon as she snuggled him against her chin.

Lady Maeve looked equally delighted with her kitten. "Are they not too young to be away from their mother?"

"They were weaned soon before we left. There are four more at home, but Patience would not let me bring them all," Joy said as though Patience were daft.

"Why do you not go with her to take them out, my lady?"

"But the bruises," she whispered in return, as if the entire estate was unaware she'd been gone and then rescued.

"'Tis nothing a bonnet will not hide. Fresh air will do you good," Grace reassured her, then turned to Joy while Lady Maeve decided. "There are stable boys named Paddy and Barry who I assured could help with the kittens as well. They helped me with Theo on the ship. Can you make sure they see them?"

"Of course."

Grace handed Theo back to her. Meanwhile, Maeve was already tying on a bonnet. Grace suspected Joy and the kittens would be quite good for her.

"You will speak to your sister about England?" Lady Maeve asked before they left.

"Are you coming back with us? Capital!" Joy exclaimed.

"I will do that at once." *As well as beg her to leave as soon as possible.* At least Grace could help someone else recover their happiness, even if hers was sorely injured along with her pride.

∽

RONAN FELT as though he'd been thrashed. As though someone had ripped out his heart, stamped on it, then poorly sewn it back in. The look on Grace's face and her words would haunt him forever, but he still knew it was what was best for her. When the time came to speak, he knew he had to let her go.

He would talk with Major Stuart and his wife, as well as pen a letter to Westwood. As he'd returned from a long walk of trying to sort through his thoughts and feelings, he had been surprised to see Maeve with Joy, playing with the kittens. The sound of her laughter had made him temporarily forget his own sombre mood. He rejoiced that she appeared to have found a friend to help her instead of sulking in her chambers.

Ronan found Major Stuart with his wife in one of the drawing rooms. They had been served what looked like a light meal, as it was now past noon.

"Pardon my intrusion, but may I speak with you?"

"Of course," Major Stuart said and began to stand up. Ronan waved him back down.

"Would you care for some tea?" Mrs. Stuart asked.

"No, thank you. I wish to speak with you both about Miss Grace." Something that had been put off with the necessity of dealing with Maeve's rescue first.

Ronan was aware of Patience Stuart stiffening her posture. Was it his tone of voice? Was she opposed to her sister being forced to wed him? Even though he agreed, it still chafed.

"About that," Major Stuart began. "I think the crisis has been averted, since we managed to depart shortly after your ship. There was enough chaos and confusion that Westwood was certain he could smooth things over."

Ronan agreed and nodded. It was what was best for Grace. "You will, of course, let me know if word has spread?"

"Of course," they agreed quickly but dismissively.

"We thought we would depart in the morning if you have no objection."

Ronan tried to keep the surprise from his face. He had a great many objections, but he kept them to himself. "I am certain you are all anxious to be home, though please do not feel the need to hurry away on our account. I am sure Maeve would enjoy the company. In fact, I have just seen her making friends with Miss Joy and the kittens in the stable yard."

"About your sister…Grace has just been in here and suggested we take Lady Maeve to London with us. She thought it might be a nice diversion for her—where she can heal, away from reminders of what happened here. While the Season has not yet begun, she may make a few acquaintances. Then, if she wishes to remain, she may be brought out under the patronage of a duchess and a viscountess. Joy will also be making her début."

His initial instinct was to shout, 'No!' He didn't want everything to be happening so quickly. He needed time to make sense of all that was happening. Ronan knew the plan was a brilliant one, yet he wanted to keep Maeve here to protect her and wrap her in cotton wool, but that was a ridiculous notion as he had failed to do that already. She would heal much faster away from all the reminders of her spectacular misadventure. "I have no objection if my parents are agreeable. I think they will be relieved, as my mother has been afraid to leave my father in order to take her to London."

"Joy will be delighted to have someone to share the experience with her. She is rather dreading Society," Patience added with a wry twist of her lips.

"I will speak with my parents about the matter. By the by, my father requests you join him at dinner this evening to show his appreciation for your help last evening."

"We should be honoured to meet him," Major Stuart said, "if it is not too much for his health."

"It will give him great pleasure as well as be good for him, I suspect."

The Stuarts nodded.

"Please make yourselves at home here, even though the stay will be short. There are fine paths for riding and some excellent cattle to choose from should you wish to see more of Ireland."

He took his leave and went to tell his mother about Maeve's invitation, even though he'd rather retreat and nurse his wounds. Ronan already felt the loss of Grace as keenly as though he himself had laid her on the altar of sacrifice.

The great hall of Donnellan Castle had not seen such activity in years. The long table, polished to a dull gleam and adorned with flickering candelabra, groaned under the weight of a veritable feast: roasted meats, fragrant pies, steaming bowls of vegetables, and an array of sauces and delicacies. Fires roared in the hearths, casting a warm glow over the ancient tapestries and high ceiling. It was an evening meant for celebration, though the mood was yet sombre, the events of the past days lingering in the air.

The party had gathered there, and Ronan found it difficult to keep his eyes from Grace. She'd borrowed a gown from Maeve and he wondered how he'd not noticed her radiance before.

Ronan watched as his father made his entrance with innate authority, his cane tapping rhythmically against the stone floor. Though his frame was gaunt and his steps cautious, he was still every inch the lord of the manor. His lady walked beside him, gently guiding and steadying. Ronan had helped his father downstairs some time before dinner was to begin so he would be spared the indignity of being witnessed in needing help.

All those present came forward as his father approached the head of the table, and he gestured for them to be seated. "Let us not stand on ceremony tonight," he said, his deep voice carrying a note of wry amusement. "I am too old, and you are too young."

As they took their places, Grace was seated between Lord Donnellan and Lady Maeve, a position that seemed to disconcert her. Ronan knew she disliked being the centre of attention.

He watched as his father's sharp gaze swept over the table, pausing on Grace with unmistakable interest. "So, you are the young lady to whom we owe our gratitude," he said, his eyes glinting with curiosity.

Grace inclined her head, and she inhaled deeply before answering. "I did very little, my lord."

"Little?" he repeated, his brow lifting. "My dear, you saved my daughter and very likely my son as well. If this is what you call little, I should love to know what is much to you."

"Father," Ronan interjected, his tone dry, "perhaps you might allow Miss Whitford to enjoy her meal before overwhelming her?"

Lord Donnellan's lips twitched in what might have been a smile. "Nonsense. A young lady brave enough to steal my daughter out from under Flynn's roof can surely endure a few words from an old man."

"Nevertheless," Grace said with quiet humour, "I find your praise far more daunting than Flynn's threats, my lord."

A ripple of laughter passed around the table, and Ronan saw Grace's shoulders ease slightly. Maeve leaned towards her, whispering not so quietly in a confiding manner. "He likes you. Not many people achieve that on their first meeting."

Grace smiled, though Ronan could tell she'd rather observe than speak.

"And how are you finding Donnellan Castle, Miss Whitford?" Lady Donnellan asked kindly.

"It is beautiful," Grace replied earnestly. "The history here feels alive. I can almost imagine medieval knights and their ladies filling these halls."

"Knights and ladies," Maeve said with a smile. "While the reality is drafts and bats."

Everyone at the table laughed, and even Maeve's subdued chuckle joined the chorus.

"Before we begin, I should like to make a toast." Lord Donnellan lifted his glass and everyone else followed. "Whilst we do not celebrate our enemy's death, we are very grateful that the feud has been brought to an end, and to have Maeve back where she belongs."

Ronan was grateful to see the light back in his father's eyes.

"We give thanks, too, for the bravery of this lovely young lady..." He lifted his glass to Grace. "and for the quick actions of Major Stuart."

"Hear, hear!" They all lifted their glasses and drank.

His mother signalled to the footmen, who came forward to begin serving.

"We should hold a ball," his father announced, continuing in the vein of celebration.

"It might seem rather callous with Flynn not cold in the ground," Ronan warned.

"We must celebrate somehow." His father was almost pouting. It seemed that now he had come out of his chambers, he meant to resume living again. For that, Ronan was grateful.

"This will have to do as they will be leaving on the morrow," Maeve said.

"Is this true?" he asked Grace.

"I am afraid so, my lord."

"Then we shall make the most of the time we have together. I hope it will not be the last, however." He cast a meaningful look between Ronan and Grace. Ronan felt his father might as well have pierced his heart with a dagger, for it was of little use to him now. It would be leaving on the ship for England tomorrow.

CHAPTER 18

The voyage back to England was a far cry from the tense and tumultuous journey to Ireland. The seas were calm, and no gales or superstitious sailors threatened her person. Grace sat and watched the days go by while trying to determine how the world could look outwardly so calm when inside she felt overturned and empty.

Around her, life continued as though nothing had changed. The others filled the days with easy chatter. The ever lively Joy had taken to entertaining Lady Maeve with tales of their escapades in England, embellished to such a degree that even Maeve managed to forget her troubles and laugh. Mr. Cunningham joined in the merriment as usual. The kittens proved an endless source of amusement, tumbling over each other in pursuit of Joy's ribbons and drawing laughter from all corners of the deck.

Lady Maeve appeared to be recovering quickly. The sea air seemed to agree with her, and as the bruises faded so did her reticence. Grace could not help but feel a sense of obligation to her—this young woman who had endured so much. Yet Maeve was also a painful reminder of her brother, with those piercing eyes and shining black locks. From there her mind created memories of Ronan's intense gaze, and the unbridgeable distance that now yawned between them.

Once back in England, Grace moved through her days like a shadow of herself. No one mentioned the ordeal, as if it had never existed. Most of her days were spent in the gardens despite the cold, staring at nothing. Even reading had lost its allure.

It was during one of these moments of reflection that the Dowager Viscountess Lady Westwood approached in her wheeled chair. She was a fragile-appearing woman with sharp eyes that missed nothing, and she carried herself with a grace that belied her age. Without preamble, she stopped beside Grace, her gloved hands folded neatly in her lap.

"You look as though you've lost something, Grace," the Dowager Viscountess said, her tone light but pointed.

Grace blinked, startled out of her reverie. "I beg your pardon, my lady?"

"You have been wandering about like a ghost since your return," the Dowager continued. "It is most unbecoming in a young woman to mope, especially one with so much life ahead of her."

Grace flushed, lowering her gaze. "I apologize if I have been remiss in my conduct."

"Do not mistake me," the Dowager said briskly. "I am not trying to scold you, Grace, but I find it curious that a young lady who showed such courage and resourcefulness to rescue the young maiden…"

Grace looked up sharply.

"Oh, yes, I have heard it all. But you are behaving as though you have left something behind in Ireland."

Grace's hands twisted in her lap. "I do not know what you mean."

"Do you not?" the Dowager's sharp gaze seemed to pierce through her. "Perhaps I am mistaken, but I suspect that your heart is more disquieted than you would care to admit."

Grace opened her mouth to protest, but the elder woman waved her hand dismissively. "I shall not pry, my dear, but take it from someone who has lived long enough to know better—when one's heart is wounded, it is best to address it straight away rather than let it fester. Find that courage again, my dear. Do come in from the cold soon."

Before Grace could respond, the Dowager turned and rolled away, leaving Grace to grapple with her thoughts in silence. "'Tis all very well, but he does not want me. How am I supposed to face the pain with courage when he made it clear there was nothing between us?"

Yet she knew the Dowager was right. She could not allow herself to waste away, pining for something that could never be.

She went inside, the warmth of the house enveloping her. Her limbs began prickling as the warmth infused her body. How long had she been out there? Chafing her hands together, she went to find her sisters for advice. Perhaps keeping busy would keep her thoughts from straying to Carew. She stopped short of entering the drawing room, however, when she overheard them discussing her.

"I have just come from speaking with Grace," she heard the Dowager say. "I may have been too harsh with her."

"You have noticed it as well. I have tried to give her time, but it is clear something is wrong," Patience's voice added. "She has endured so much, from the unexpected journey alone and then witnessing Flynn's death. She is more tender-hearted than I when it comes to those things."

"I do not think that is it at all, my dear."

"You think she is heartsick for Carew?"

"I suspect that is very much the case. Even I knew she was taken with him during her first Season. Who would not be? Even at my age, a roguish look from those blue eyes makes my heart palpitate," spoken with wry amusement.

"She did mention having feelings for him." Grace could hear the dismay in Patience's voice. "But I saw no signs of an attachment while we were there. I thought they parted amicably."

"My dear, I am not sure you see anything besides dear Ashley at the moment."

"Perhaps so." Patience sounded amused. "But why did she not say anything?"

"Perhaps she did not wish to put a damper on your own happiness. And with Carew's sister present…it is not Grace's way."

Grace hated that they were speaking of her heartache so openly, but if no one besides Maeve had seen an attachment on Carew's part, then it must have been a figment of her imagination. Had Carew kissed her out of pity?

The thought made her cheeks burn with shame. He had been kind to her, yes, but he had made no promises. He had not played the rogue. He had simply…been. Even so, he had no intention of offering for her. It was time to put him out of her mind.

"Since a scandal has been averted, Westwood does not wish for the attachment. Of course, he knows Carew better than anyone and he thinks Grace would do better with someone more suited to her," the Dowager continued.

Grace wondered how well anyone actually knew her at all. Carew was the only one who had ever turned her head, and the thought of facing a third Season of looking for a match was enough to send her spirits plummeting further into the abyss. She might as well tell Westwood to arrange something for her and save herself the trouble, though spinsterhood was looking more and more appealing by the moment. She was now an aunt, and could be as doting and as eccentric as she liked.

"Sometimes I think Grace is the most innocent of us all," Patience remarked.

"Where Carew is the most experienced? I do not know, my dear, but Grace sees something in him and it should be her decision."

"Perhaps," Patience said again, sounding hesitant.

"Now come, Patience. Just because she is not as outspoken as you does not mean she is not entitled to her own opinions and choices."

"You are right, of course, but is it wrong for me to want to protect her?"

Grace's heart squeezed. She felt the same about her sisters.

"I fear it may be too late for that, but perhaps you can see to helping her find her way through this maze." The Dowager's wisdom was much needed, Grace mused, although she hated to hear herself discussed so. Nonetheless, she knew they were worried for her.

"Should we send for Faith and Hope? Maybe having everyone together would buoy her spirits."

"I have spoken to her. Let us see if she rallies."

Her family meant well, but there was much they did not understand. Yet she could not bring herself to tell them all that had happened. Perhaps it was for the best to keep it to herself since it meant so little to Carew. However, the experience had changed her, for better or worse.

Grace turned and walked quietly back to her room, where Theo was bathing himself in the sunlight on the chair by the window. Stretched out on his back with his paws covering his face, it was hard not to smile at the creature. She stroked his soft fur, and his purrs began immediately without even opening his eyes. To be able to love and trust so unconditionally…that settled it. She would replace Carew in her heart with a dozen cats. Would that be enough?

∼

IT HAD BEEN four weeks and one day since they had left. Ronan could not help but count the days. He'd spent all day and half of every night working with the horses. There was a soothing simplicity to their needs. A horse did not obscure its intentions behind a veil of civility or pretence. Though their wills could be a battle, he welcomed the challenge. His thoughts could not waver when breaking a horse, and so it was his chosen remedy. Exhaustion was the best remedy for a broken heart. When he worked until his muscles burned and his head ached from the sun, there was little energy left for thoughts of Grace Whitford. His mind had not yet learned to control his dreams, however. Eventually, he'd hear of Grace's betrothal to some worthy gentleman, and then he'd suffer anew. It was no less than he deserved as penance for his sins.

"Are you finished for now, me lord?" Paddy, the stable hand, approached and took the reins of the gelding Ronan had been working with. The boy jerked his head towards the paddock fence, where Ronan's mother stood watching him, her face shadowed with concern.

Ronan sighed, removed his hat, and wiped the sweat from his brow. "Mother," he greeted her as he approached. "What brings you out here?"

"It is the only way to have a word with you these days," she replied, her tone carrying a note of reproach.

"Is something amiss? Has something happened to Father?" Ronan asked, straightening instinctively.

"Your father is quite well, actually," she said, and Ronan noted a hint of satisfaction in her tone. Even the stable hands had spoken of his lordship leaving his chambers regularly, a marked improvement from his previous seclusion.

"I have received a letter from England," she continued, holding out an envelope. "I thought you might wish to read it."

Ronan eyed the letter warily. "A summary from you will do just as well."

"I think not," she said firmly, thrusting the letter closer. "You have never been a coward, Ronan."

He sighed and took the letter from her, his fingers hesitating on the seal. "You deserve to be happy," she said softly. "Whatever you think your past has made you, it also made you the man you are now. That does not mean you must sacrifice the one you love as a penance."

Ronan's gaze drifted to the pastures, where the horses grazed in peace. "I have already told her to find someone else worthy."

His mother tilted her head, her brow arching in mild challenge. "Did you decide this for her, or did you deign to ask her what she wanted?"

"'Tis not so simple, Mother."

"Is it not?"

Ronan opened his mouth to reply but found no words. The unspoken answer hung between them. He could not answer that.

Changing approach, she said, "Will you join us for church today?"

"Us?"

"Your father wishes to attend services. Since it has been years since he felt like going, I thought perhaps you and I could also make the effort."

Ronan frowned, caught by surprise. "I had forgotten it was Sunday."

"Well, remember now. If your father wishes to leave the castle, we should rejoice."

His mother turned and left him to the letter.

Reluctantly, he opened it and read.

My dearest Mama,

I hope this letter finds you in good health and spirits, and to reassure you I am recovering well. The journey here was uneventful. The Channel holds little beauty to the Irish Sea, though I will admit the cliffs in Sussex rival our own. England has its own charm, though it is very different from the beauty of Donnellan.

Now that I am safely ensconced in Westwood House, London, I can admit to buoying spirits and the wisdom of healing in a new place. London is bustling with a liveliness that is almost dizzying, and the people are as varied as they are fascinating. It is never quiet here. I am slowly beginning to feel at ease, and my hosts are everything that is good. Your absence is keenly felt, though I have been fortunate to find new friendships here that make the days brighter.

Miss Joy Whitford has been a constant delight. She is, without doubt, the most lively and enchanting person I have ever met. She possesses a spirit that refuses to be dimmed, a quality that I find both inspiring and infectious. She has taken it upon herself to befriend me, and I must confess I have rarely laughed so freely. Whether it is some unintentional mischief or the antics of her kittens, there is always something to draw a smile.

Yet, even in the midst of such liveliness, not all are happy. Miss Grace carries a sadness that she cannot hide from those who care for her. They are concerned about her. Even I find her changed from our brief acquaintance at Donnellan. She is as kind and thoughtful as ever, but her smiles are few, and her laughter seems to belong more to memory than to the present. I wish I could lighten her heart as Joy has lightened mine, but I find myself at a loss. There are moments when I catch her gazing out of the window, or she sits in the gardens alone. I wonder what thoughts keep her so. It is clear that she is struggling with some sorrow, though she does not speak of it. Forgive me if this is impertinent, but please tell Ronan I think perhaps she misses him.

I wish to be of what comfort I can, though I know I cannot replace what she feels she has lost. Joy and I have often sought to include her in our little amusements, but I suspect she finds more solace in solitude than in our chatter. Still, I hope that, in time, her spirits will lift. I wish to help her as she helped me, though I suspect I remind her of who she longs for.

Please give my love to all at home, and be reassured I am well. Though I am far away, my heart remains with you, and I think of you often and do wish you could share this with me.

Your ever loving daughter,
Maeve

THE CHAPEL WAS ANCIENT, its stone walls warmed by shafts of sunlight streaming through the high, arched windows. Ronan sat beside his mother and father, feeling an unusual weight in the simplicity of the moment while reflecting on Maeve's words about Grace. Could it be she mourned for him as he did for her? His father, though still frail, sat upright with a strength Ronan had not seen in years. The sight brought a pang of something—pride, perhaps, or hope.

After the hymns were sung, the vicar took to the pulpit, his measured gaze sweeping over the congregation before he began. "I wish to speak on something we often overlook," he announced, his voice calm but commanding. "Grace."

Ronan's breath stilled in his chest. The word struck him like a physical blow, and though he knew it was irrational, he felt as though every eye in the room had turned to him. The vicar continued, oblivious to Ronan's inner turmoil.

"Not everyone will agree with me," the vicar said, "but the more I learn of the Scriptures, and from His Holy Word in the New Testament writings, the more I believe it to be the truth. Works and deeds are an outward manifestation of our love, but nothing we do ourselves will save us. It is only by grace."

Ronan could not stop the words echoing over and over in his mind and heart. *Only by Grace.*

"Grace can be hard to accept," the vicar went on. "We judge ourselves unworthy and feel we must be perfect, but this is not what the Scriptures tell us is necessary."

He paused, then quoted with quiet reverence, "For it is written in the second book of Corinthians: *And He said unto me, My grace is sufficient for thee: for My strength is made perfect in weakness.* So, brethren, forgive yourself and accept His grace, for God will forgive you."

Ronan's jaw tightened and he looked down at his hands, clasped together in his lap. The words reverberated through him, disturbing in their simplicity. Was that not precisely what he had refused to do? He had judged himself unworthy—not only of forgiveness but of Grace herself.

He heard very little after that, ruminating on the vicar's words. Could it be possible? Was there still hope for him? Hope for him and Grace?

After the service, the congregation gathered outside the chapel, exchanging pleasantries and offering kind words to Lord Donnellan, who greeted everyone pleasantly. Ronan mustered his control through this ordeal even though his impatience to be gone was growing by the minute.

"Ronan," his mother said, catching his elbow as they made their way back to the carriage. "If that wasn't a sign, I do not know what could be more plain. For once, do something for yourself."

"It is obvious to anyone with eyes that you love that lass," his father interjected, surprising him.

Ronan hesitated, the weight of his father's words pressing against the doubts he had carried for weeks. "She deserves better than I," he murmured. "A man without so many sins to his name."

"Nonsense," his father said sharply. "Do you think I did not feel the same when I courted your mother? She was as stubborn as she was beautiful, and I was nothing more than a young lord with too much pride and not enough sense. I had to fight tooth and nail for her favour—prove myself worthy of her in every way."

Ronan blinked in surprise. "You have never told me that."

"Because it mattered not once I had her," Lord Donnellan said, his gaze softening. "But let me tell you this, Ronan: I would have moved mountains for that woman, and I still would. If you feel the same for Grace then you had better stop wallowing in self-doubt and go and get her."

Ronan's chest tightened, his father's words cutting through his defences like a blade. "Mayhap I have already ruined my chance."

Lord Donnellan fixed him with a stern look. "Then work twice as hard to win her back. Prove to her that you are the man she deserves. 'Tis not about being perfect, lad—'tis about being willing."

Ronan said nothing, his thoughts too tangled for speech. But as the carriage began its slow journey back to the castle, the weight of the vicar's words and his parent's insistence bore down on him. Perhaps it was time to stop running—from himself, from his past, and from the possibility of something greater than his fears.

CHAPTER 19

Another day and Grace had survived. Tonight was to be Joy and Lady Maeve's first official ball. The ballroom glittered with the golden glow of candlelight, their light refracted through crystal chandeliers that hung like jewels from the ceiling. Garlands of autumn greenery were strung from the ceiling, sprays of flower arrangements lined the walls, and ribbons were strewn about. The polished floors gleamed, reflecting the swirling colours of gowns and the rhythmic movement of dancing couples. The orchestra played a lively reel, filling the room, mingling with the hum of conversation and bursts of laughter.

The ladies in their silks and satins spun like samaras falling through the air. Jewel-toned gowns of emerald green, sapphire blue, and ruby red adorned the matrons, while the more delicate hues of lavender, rose, and cream lent an air of soft elegance to the young misses. Grace herself wore a gown of sea green, its modest design enhanced by lace trimmings and a strand of pearls. The effect was understated but elegant, as Grace preferred.

Joy, on the other hand, was the very picture of unrestrained exuberance. Her gown of lavender shimmered as she spun across the floor, her laughter ringing out above the music as she danced with

Mr. Cunningham. Undaunted by Joy's unbridled enthusiasm, he matched her steps with surprising ease and an easy laughter. They were a captivating pair, their gaiety a stark contrast from the more subdued dancers around them. Instead of the *ton* frowning at the lack of decorum, they looked indulgently upon Joy. She had that effect on others.

Grace observed them with a faint smile, though her heart still ached. She had attended several engagements this past week, smiled at every compliment, and danced with a cheerfulness she did not feel. It was an effort not to let her true feelings show, and though she succeeded outwardly, it took its toll. Several gentlemen, encouraged by her politeness, had begun to pay her marked attention. Perhaps that was all they required—a willing smile—but for Grace it felt unnatural.

Lady Maeve, at least, was faring better, and for that Grace was deeply relieved. It was a joy to see her take tentative steps towards reclaiming the vivacious spirit Carew had so fondly described. The bruises that once marked her skin had faded, and though there was a subtle hesitancy in her gaze at times, it was clear she was beginning to be herself again. Joy had befriended her, and it was difficult to remain subdued near her zest for life.

The evening's ball was proof enough of her transformation. Lady Maeve, dressed in a gown of soft ivory silk that complemented her dark hair and bright eyes, was the very picture of exotic beauty. Her shy smiles lit up her face whenever a gentleman approached her, captivating her partners. She had quickly become the toast of the evening.

Grace watched with a mixture of admiration and wistfulness as one gentleman after another sought Maeve's hand for a dance. There was an ease to her manner that had been absent when they first arrived in England. As the strains of a lively country dance began, she was partnered by Lord Ravensfield, who was known for his good humour. He was a charming, handsome gentleman who was much sought after. His tall, broad-shouldered frame and easy smile made him a favourite among the ladies.

They stepped onto the dance floor, Maeve's silk skirts flowing with each movement, her cheeks faintly flushed with exertion and delight. Grace noted the way Maeve's laughter bubbled up as he murmured something to her during a turn. It was a sound so free and unguarded that Grace felt her heart ache with a bittersweet mixture of joy and sorrow.

She could not help but wonder if Maeve's heart had truly been affected by Flynn. Could anyone fully recover from such pain? Could a love lost ever feel whole once more?

Grace sighed inwardly. She doubted it. Love, when true, left its mark. Time might dull the pain, but it could not erase it. She hoped Maeve would come to see that true love did not abuse—it cherished. Flynn had been a fraud, and Maeve deserved someone true.

But as for Grace herself? She knew it would be a long time before her heart could open to another. Was it unfair, then, to allow these gentlemen to hope? Did they expect no more than a compliant, accommodating wife? Staying busy helped to distract her, but it did little to quiet her thoughts. Each dance partner only reminded her of the one man she could not forget. Compared to Carew, everyone else paled in comparison.

If only he had done something truly horrendous to me, she thought wryly, *it might be easier to let him go*. But no, Ronan had been the perfect gentleman—respectful and honourable. How was she to harden her heart against that?

As Grace observed her surroundings, she did not notice Mr. George Lynton approaching until he stood directly in front of her. His bow was impeccable, his smile warm but tinged with a hint of nervousness. "Miss Whitford," he said smoothly, "may I have the honour of this dance?"

Caught by surprise, Grace blinked, but her manners asserted themselves quickly. "Of course, Mr. Lynton," she replied, allowing him to help her to her feet. His hand was steady as it guided her, and though she did not particularly feel inclined to dance, she appreciated his genuine kindness.

As they took their places on the floor, Grace noted how Mr.

Lynton's attire, whilst not ostentatious, bore the quiet marks of a gentleman of means. His dark coat was finely tailored, and his neckcloth arranged with just enough flair to suggest a man who paid attention to detail. The orchestra began the next song, and Mr. Lynton led her into the steps with a grace that belied his otherwise understated manner.

"Miss Whitford?"

She started, realizing she had been neglecting her partner. "Forgive me," she said quickly. "My mind wandered."

"A true testament to your dancing skills, then," her partner replied with a twinkle in his eyes. Mr. Lynton was a pleasant man with a warm smile and an easy charm. "I must mind my steps, lest I tumble us across the floor and create a domino effect of the other couples."

She smiled at his good humour, though it was faint. "Somehow, I doubt that," she said lightly. "It is only because you are so accomplished that my mind strayed."

"Would you care to tell me about him?"

Grace's cheeks warmed, and she stumbled slightly. "I beg your pardon?"

Mr. Lynton chuckled, his gaze kind. "There is no shame in it, Miss Whitford. It is clear someone has your heart."

Grace's cheeks heated. Was she so obvious? Apparently so.

"It is nothing to be ashamed of."

"Even when I make a fool of myself over it?" she asked, her tone wry.

"Even then. But you have not done so, I assure you. It is only because I recognize the same affliction in myself."

Grace blinked, taken aback. "Oh," she said softly. "Is there any hope for you?"

Mr. Lynton smiled sadly. "I am afraid not. My affliction married another."

"I am sorry," Grace said sincerely.

"And you?" he asked, his voice gentler. "Do you think there is hope for you?"

"He is not yet wed," she admitted, her voice quiet, "but I was given a speech which left me in no doubt of his intent."

He arched a brow. "Ah, the one where he becomes a martyr? That you deserve better, that you are too good, and he is unworthy?"

Grace gave a soft huff of surprise. "Just so. I had not considered it in that light."

Mr. Lynton's expression grew serious. "Anyone who does not take advantage of the heart you offer does not deserve you, Miss Whitford."

Grace smiled faintly, though that organ still ached. "If only my mind and heart would think in unison."

"When your heart heals," Mr. Lynton said with a small smile, "perhaps we could deal well together. There are worse foundations for marriage than fondness and friendship."

Grace tilted her head thoughtfully. "I fear, if that were the case, our poets would be sadly lacking for inspiration."

"Indeed," he replied, laughing softly.

The music slowed, signalling the end of the dance. Mr. Lynton bowed over her hand with courtly grace before escorting her back to her sisters. As Grace took her seat beside Maeve, her gaze flickered briefly to the sparkling chandeliers above. For a moment, she allowed herself the smallest flicker of hope—that one day her heart might mend.

∼

RONAN STOOD JUST beyond the grand archway, remaining in the shadows afforded by the towering marble columns. It took but a moment for his searching gaze to find Grace, and everything else faded to a blur in the periphery. She danced near the centre of the room, her pale green gown flowing like a quiet ripple of water among the more vivid hues of the other ladies. Her smile was captivating, her expression serene as she conversed with her dance partner—a gentleman who, though well-dressed and polished, seemed entirely unworthy of the privilege of her company. Ronan's chest tightened at the sight, a mixture of longing and jealousy warring within him.

Grace laughed at some remark her partner made, and Ronan felt an ache so deep it nearly brought him to his knees. He wanted to bring that smile to her face. She was everything he had missed, everything he had tried to convince himself he could live without—the calming presence, the quiet strength that soothed his restless soul. The sight of her was worth riding day and night to reach her.

And yet here she was, seemingly flourishing without him, whilst he had been left feeling as though a piece of himself had been carved away. Had Maeve been mistaken?

Ronan's hands clenched at his sides. It took every ounce of his considerable fortitude not to stride onto the ballroom floor and steal her from her partner. He longed to sweep her into his arms, to demand she listen to the torrent of emotions he had buried for weeks. But he did not have that right. He had let her go.

Instead, he stood rooted to the spot, waiting and watching until the dance concluded. His pulse quickened as the strains of a waltz began to play, and he held his breath, hoping against hope that her dance was not already spoken for.

When her eyes finally met his, the world seemed to still. Grace froze for the briefest moment, her serene expression giving way to one of shock. A mixture of pain and joy flickered across her face, her composure faltering as she glanced down, then back up, as though she could not quite believe what she was seeing. Ronan's heart leaped and then sank. He had caused that pain, that hesitation, and now it was his burden to make amends.

He stepped forward, weaving through the crowd with resolute determination. He reached her just as her previous partner bowed politely and stepped away.

"May I have this dance?" he asked, his voice low, almost unsteady.

Grace hesitated, her lips parting as though to refuse. But then she nodded, placing her gloved hand in his.

Ronan led her to the dance floor, his hand resting lightly on her waist as they began to move. The music swelled around them, but all

Ronan could hear was the pounding of his own heart. She was so close that her familiar scent teased his senses, her touch filled the missing piece of him.

He considered making a light remark, perhaps even a jest, "Did you miss me?" but the words died on his tongue. Instead, he found himself consumed by the sheer relief of being near her again. The hollow ache in his chest seemed to lessen, his heart feeling whole for the first time in weeks.

The strain between them was palpable, a weight that neither seemed able to lift. As they began to move in time with the music, Ronan allowed himself to study her, his gaze tracing the delicate curve of her cheek and the soft sweep of her lashes. She was as lovely as he remembered, but there was a faint shadow beneath her eyes that hinted at restless nights and unspoken worries. The smile she had worn earlier, so bright and engaging, was now subdued, as though it had been a mask she had grown weary of holding in place.

Ronan forced himself to break the silence even though he was content to drink her in. "I am not sure what it says about me that my eyes found you and no other."

Grace's expression softened, and she looked back up at him, uncertain of his sincerity.

"How is Maeve?"

"She is faring well, it seems," she said gently. "Joy has been a great source of diversion for her, and the change of scenery seems to have done her good. She laughs often now, though I think her heart is still mending."

Ronan nodded, relief mingling with guilt as her words sank in. "It seems I am in your continued debt."

"Nonsense," Grace said firmly. "Maeve is strong, and she is recovering in her own way. It takes time."

He hesitated, his grip on her waist tightening slightly as he searched for the right words. "I have carried much guilt for what happened to her," he admitted.

"Maeve does not blame you," Grace said, her voice steady. "I think she is struggling to forgive herself."

Ronan fell silent, her words striking something deep within him. It no longer felt as if they were discussing Maeve. Perhaps she spoke of herself as well. The dance continued and he held her gaze as they crossed the floor, their movements perfectly together, though his thoughts were anything but orderly.

"Can you forgive me for being a fool?" he asked, his voice almost drowned out by the music.

Grace looked up at him, her expression unreadable. "You let me go," she repeated softly, her voice tinged with hurt.

The words hung in the air between them. For a moment, Grace seemed surprised by her own words. Her cheeks flushed, and she glanced away, her composure slipping further. Ronan cursed himself silently, unsure of what had possessed him to speak so plainly.

"I thought it was the for the best," he continued, his jaw tightening as he struggled to regain control of his wayward thoughts. "I thought I was sparing you—giving you the chance to find someone better. Someone who could give you the life you deserve."

"And yet here you are," Grace said softly, her gaze returning to his. There was no malice in her tone, only quiet curiosity. "Why? What has changed?"

"Let us just say that a higher power opened my eyes. I know I am far from perfect, and you still deserve a better man than I, but if you can see your way to forgive me…" he said simply, his voice trailing off, raw with emotion. He shook his head. "I fear my words are often inept when I most wish them to matter."

"Please continue, nevertheless."

She did not wish to make this easy on him. Very well. "I thought I could live without you, Grace, but I was wrong. I have been wrong about many things, but never more so than this."

Grace blinked with surprise as her steps faltered slightly. Ronan adjusted instantly, steadying her without missing a beat.

"You don't have to say anything now," he said hurriedly. "I know I don't deserve your forgiveness. But I could not let you think—could not let you believe—that I did not care about you."

"I never doubted that you cared," Grace said, her voice steady now.

"But caring is not the same as choosing me." She looked away then, her lashes lowering as a faint blush rose to her cheeks in response to her boldness.

The truth of her words cut through him like a blade. "I am here now," he said, his voice fierce with conviction. "And I will not make the mistake of letting you go again—no matter how long it takes to prove it to you."

The music swelled to its crescendo, and they came to a halt as the final notes faded. Ronan bowed low over her hand, his eyes never leaving hers. "Will you forgive me, Grace?"

The words hung in the air between them, and for a moment, Grace seemed at a loss for a reply. Her blush deepened, and she glanced away, her composure faltering ever so slightly. Ronan cursed himself silently, unsure of what had possessed him to speak so plainly. He need not force the issue here and now. He should have waited until they were not in a public place and wooed her more gently, but his heart was on his sleeve, and he'd held his feelings in for so long he'd wanted to right his wrongs as quickly as possible.

"I do not know." She slipped from his grasp then and left the floor.

Ronan watched her go, cursing his impatience.

He sought out his sister for a dance to ensure she was thriving, then left, needing time to consider his strategy.

CHAPTER 20

The cold autumn air enveloped Grace as she stepped onto the terrace, the sounds of the ball muffled by the heavy curtains she had slipped past. The stone balustrade was cold beneath her fingers, a blessed reprieve from the heat and press of the crowded ballroom. She exhaled slowly, her breath curling into the chilly air.

When Grace had first spotted Carew across the glittering expanse of the ballroom, everything had faded into the background as her gaze locked on his tall, commanding figure. Thank goodness she had not been dancing or she would have faltered. He'd stood near the entrance, his dark coat impeccably tailored, while his blue eyes scanned the room with an intensity that seemed to pierce through the shimmering haze of candlelight and silk.

Her first reaction was disbelief—it had to be a mirage. Yet there he was, looking every inch the enigmatic lord she had tried so hard to forget. His presence was undeniable, a magnetism that seemed to draw her attention no matter how fiercely she willed herself to look away.

Conflicting emotions flooded her chest, each one vying for dominance. There was joy at the sight of him—whole, hale, and here—but it was swiftly tempered by the ache of hurt, the memory of his dismissal, his insistence that she find someone 'worthy'. Anger simmered beneath the surface, though it was directed as much at herself as at him. Would his presence always have the power to unmoor her?

It had felt like Moses parting the Red Sea as he'd walked towards her and solicited her hand.

Unfortunately, she had been unprepared and had reacted poorly. What had she done? It was everything she had hoped for this past month, yet she had fled the ballroom as soon as the waltz ended. She was too disturbed by the maelstrom of emotions that had surfaced during their conversation. He'd spoken every word she'd longed to hear, so why did she mistrust them?

Despite Grace's wish to flee, she could not spoil the evening for Maeve and Joy. They deserved to laugh and dance without her melancholy casting a shadow over their happiness, so she hid amongst the dowagers and chaperones until the evening ended.

As they returned home in the carriage, Maeve and Joy filled the silence with chatter, while the Dowager and Grace listened. Maeve's eyes sparkled as she recounted her dances, her laughter light and carefree.

"Did you see me trip during the quadrille?" Joy exclaimed, giggling. "I nearly took Lady Abernathy down with me!"

Maeve joined in the laughter, her cheeks glowing. "And yet you recovered so earnestly, poor dear. I could not help but admire your determination."

Joy then launched into a particularly dramatic retelling of an incident during the reel. "Did you see," she exclaimed, flinging her hands up for effect, "just as I was about to execute the perfect turn, Mr. Cunningham stepped on my hem! I nearly toppled over Lord Dunton. His hairpiece came loose and was flailing about like a squirrel hanging on to a tree in a wind storm."

Maeve clapped her hands together, laughing so hard she could barely speak. "Joy, you are incorrigible!"

The Dowager made a noise indicating she despaired of the child.

Grace offered a faint smile but remained silent, her thoughts far from the merry conversation. Despite some time to calm herself, her thoughts remained fixed on Ronan. As they arrived home, Joy and Maeve were still chattering animatedly as they ascended the stairs, their voices trailing off into the upper floors. Grace, however, lingered in the hall, turning to bid the Dowager goodnight before making her way to her sitting room.

When she opened the door, she stopped short, her hand flying to her chest. "Faith! Hope!" she exclaimed. Her sisters were seated comfortably by the hearth, steaming cups of tea in hand, their faces lighting up as they saw her.

"Grace!" Hope set her tea-cup down and rose, only for Grace to wrap both of them in a fierce embrace. "We have missed you so!"

"And I have missed you!" Grace's voice wavered as she held them tightly. "I am so glad you have come!"

Faith smiled, smoothing back Grace's hair as she pulled away. "Patience thought you might need us. Westwood and Rotham grumbled, but they can manage for a night."

Before Grace could respond, she turned to see Patience entering with a tray of biscuits, her usual sensible demeanour mixed with concern. "Why don't we help you out of your ball gown first? And then we shall sit and talk."

Hope fetched Grace's dressing gown while Patience deftly unlaced her stays, swiftly and efficiently. Within minutes, Grace was settled into a comfortable chair by the fire, her feet curled beneath her, as Faith brushed out her hair in soothing, rhythmic strokes as they'd done every night as children.

The comfort of her sisters' presence was almost too much to bear. Tears pricked her eyes, but she blinked them away, focusing instead on the steaming cup of tea Faith pressed into her hands.

"Now," Hope said, settling herself on the rug at Grace's feet. "Tell us what has happened. We have heard bits and pieces about Ireland and Flynn, but I suspect that is not what has you so troubled tonight."

"No," Grace admitted softly, her fingers tightening around her tea-cup. "That is…to do with Lord Carew."

The sisters exchanged glances, their curiosity evident. Faith leaned forward slightly. "What has he done?"

Grace sighed, gathering her thoughts. "I thought there was something between us. In Ireland, he was different—kind, attentive—but then, before we left, he dismissed me. He told me to find someone worthy of me, as though…as though it was nothing."

Faith froze, her tea-cup halfway to her lips. "I sense there is more."

Grace hesitated, her voice faltering when she began to speak. "He came to the ball tonight. He sought me out, confessed he had made a mistake, and asked if I could forgive him."

The sisters gasped in unison, their eyes wide with astonishment.

Hope leaned closer. "What did you say?"

"I told him I did not know," Grace admitted, burying her face in her hands. "And then I left him standing there. What have I done?"

Hope moved quickly to her side, taking her hand. "You have done nothing wrong, Grace. If he truly cares for you, he will fight for you. Make him prove it."

"But is he wrong to wish for someone worthy of her?" Patience asked, ever the devil's advocate. "His intention might not have been to hurt her."

"That is the problem," Grace said quietly. "I believe he truly thought he was acting in my best interest. He wants what is best for me."

Faith set the brush down, reaching for Grace's other hand. "And what do you want?"

Grace's voice wavered as she replied, though cross at her own weakness. "I want him. Of course I do, but he caught me by surprise. I could not think clearly in the middle of a waltz."

Patience gave a rueful laugh. "No indeed, it was hardly his best choice to speak to you then. I wonder why he did not follow you when you left."

"I am very glad he did not," Grace said, feeling foolish. "I needed time to consider, yet I fear I may have bungled it. A man does have his pride, after all."

Hope shook her head. "You did not reject him outright, Grace—

did you? Besides, he came all the way from Ireland. That must surely speak for itself."

Grace's heart sank. She had not meant to be cruel, and the thought of hurting Ronan pained her deeply. "I have no wish to play such games. I cannot think what came over me."

"No one who knows you would accuse you of toying with someone's affections," Faith said firmly, "but you must decide what you want. If he speaks to you again, be honest with him."

Grace nodded slowly. Her voice, when it left her, was barely above a whisper. "I suppose I must, though I fear doubt will get the better of me."

"I am sure your courage will not fail, for does not your happiness depend upon it?" Hope asked, her tone encouraging. "Sleep upon it, dear sister. The answer will come to you."

Grace doubted she would sleep at all, her heart was too heavy with uncertainty. Yet as her sisters gathered around her, their warmth and love enveloping her like a shield, she allowed herself a small flicker of hope. They had all found love despite some very difficult circumstances.

"I am proud of you," Faith said softly. "For standing up for yourself and taking the time for reflection. You are stronger than you realize."

"And I am still a little cross with him for trying to make decisions on your behalf," Patience added, a note of indignation in her voice.

Grace managed a small smile. "As am I, in truth, but perhaps he deserves a chance to explain."

The sisters nodded in agreement, their support bolstering her resolve. Whatever the future held, Grace knew she would always have her sisters, and though he'd still not offered for her, she allowed herself to hope.

~

Ronan was relieved to hear Westwood was in Town. He was desperate to know what to do next.

"I'll announce myself if it is a good time, Hartley."

Westwood's long-time butler inclined his head as he held open the door. "Indeed. He is in his study, my lord."

Ronan strode into Westwood's study, his usual air of nonchalance had notably abandoned him. Having passed by a mirror, it showed that his neckcloth was askew, his dark coat bore the creases of having been slept in, and the shadow of stubble on his jaw spoke to a missed shave. His eyes, normally sharp and guarded, were clouded with fatigue and frustration. It mattered not if Grace would not forgive him.

"You look terrible," his old friend said from behind his desk.

"Indeed? As though I have travelled day and night from Ireland only to have my dreams crushed?"

Westwood considered him and nodded. "Yes, then," he drawled, rising slowly from his chair. "To what do I owe the honour? Although I expect we are here for the same reasons."

Ronan exhaled sharply, running a hand through his dishevelled hair. "Grace," he confirmed, his voice heavy with self-reproach.

Westwood crossed to the sideboard, where he poured a generous measure of brandy into two crystal glasses. "Sit down," he commanded, gesturing to the chair near the fire, then handed him a glass.

Ronan didn't hesitate before lowering himself into the chair with exhaustion. He accepted the brandy and took a long sip, his eyes fixed on the fire.

"Well?" Westwood prompted after a moment. "Out with it, man. What calamity has driven you to my door in such a state?"

"I've ruined everything," Ronan said bluntly, his voice cracking. "I sent her away—told her to find someone worthy, as though I were doing her a kindness. And now…now I've no idea how to win her back. She sent me away with my tail between my legs."

Westwood leaned back in his chair, his expression inscrutable. "You have come to confess your feelings, then?"

Ronan's jaw tightened. "Yes," he admitted, the words spilling out like a dam breaking. "I thought I was protecting her, sparing her from the life I might offer, but I was a fool. She is everything I've ever wanted, and I drove her away."

Westwood's lips twitched in what might have been a smile. "Well, that's a place to start. Recognizing one's mistakes is the first step to rectifying them. The second, of course, is action. Sitting here wallowing in self-pity will not win her."

Before Ronan could respond, the door opened again, and Cunningham entered, his easy grin and impeccable attire a stark contrast to Carew's dishevelled state. He paused, his sharp gaze taking in the scene, and then smirked. "Good heavens, Carew. You look as though you have just escaped from the gaol. Should I be alarmed?"

Ronan shot him a withering look. "I've no patience for your humour, Cunningham."

"Humour?" Cunningham said innocently, helping himself to a glass of brandy. "I am entirely sincere. You could frighten small children in your current state."

Westwood coughed, hiding a chuckle behind his hand. "Cunningham, perhaps now is not the time."

"Yes, do have some consideration. I am being lectured by my oldest friend."

"Why?" Cunningham waved a hand dismissively and took a seat. "What has happened? Lost your favourite horse? Or is this about Miss Whitford?"

Ronan considered his silence should be answer enough.

Cunningham's grin widened. "Ah, I see. The great Carew, undone by a lady. *How the mighty have fallen.*"

The door swung open yet again, and this time Rotham entered, his formidable presence filling the room. He took one look at Ronan and scowled. "For God's sake, Carew, what's this nonsense? Sitting here like a whipped dog, pining over a woman?"

"Rotham—" Ronan began, but the older man cut him off with a sharp gesture.

"Spare me your excuses," Rotham snapped. "You have no one to blame but yourself. If you want her, then act like it. Fight for her. Or are you content to let her slip through your fingers while you sit here brooding?"

Ronan glared at Rotham's brusqueness, but his words struck a nerve. "It's not so simple," he muttered.

"Not so simple?" Rotham echoed, his voice rising. "Nothing about women is simple. Of course not. But they are worth every bloody ounce of effort. If you care for her as much as I hear, then stop feeling sorry for yourself and do something about it."

Cunningham leaned back in his chair, swirling his brandy. "He has a point, you know. Women do like a man of action. Grand gestures, heartfelt confessions—all that romantic nonsense."

"I confessed my love for her in the middle of the ballroom last night. Does that count for nothing?" Ronan protested.

Westwood, who had been watching the exchange with open amusement, finally spoke. "The question, Carew, is whether you're willing to risk everything to try."

Ronan looked around the room, his gaze moving from Westwood to Cunningham to Rotham. Their words, though delivered in vastly different styles, carried the same message. He had made a hash of things, but maybe the path to redemption was still open.

He stood abruptly, setting his glass down with a decisive clink. "You are right," he said in a firm voice. "I have wallowed long enough. It's time to act. Have you any suggestions?"

Westwood leaned back in his chair and fixed him with a pointed look. "Winning a woman's heart requires more finesse than breaking a horse."

Ronan hesitated, his hand on the door-case. "I hardly think Grace would respond to…tactics."

"On the contrary," Westwood said smoothly, "Grace is a thoughtful young woman. A simple declaration, no matter how heartfelt, may not suffice. You have hurt her, Carew, and she'll need to see more than pretty words to believe you are sincere."

"I concur," Cunningham interjected, swirling his brandy with a casual air. "Something unexpected. Show her you're willing to go to any lengths for her."

"And do it quickly," Rotham growled, his arms crossed. "The longer you wait, the more time you give her to decide she will be the better without you. And that my wife has to dote on her, not me."

Ignoring Rotham's jest, Ronan pinched the bridge of his nose. "A grand gesture? Unexpected? What exactly do you have in mind?"

Cunningham's eyes lit up. "A serenade, perhaps? No woman can resist a heartfelt ballad sung beneath her window at midnight."

Rotham scoffed. "You'll have him arrested for a public nuisance. No, Carew needs to show her he understands her—truly understands her. Find out what she values most and prove you can give it to her."

"And what does Grace value most?" Ronan asked, exasperated.

"Family," Westwood said simply, his tone steady. "Her sisters, her home, her sense of belonging. She is not a woman who seeks wealth or power. She wants to be seen, appreciated for who she is. You must show her that you see her, that you value her as she is."

Cunningham tapped his chin thoughtfully. "You could write her a letter—perhaps poetry. A heartfelt, vulnerable one. Women adore letters. And then follow it up with something personal. Perhaps a gift?"

"A gift?" Ronan repeated, sceptical.

"Something meaningful," Cunningham clarified. "Not jewels or silks—she's not the type. A book she has mentioned loving, or a token that reminds her of your time together. Thoughtful gestures go a long way."

Rotham leaned forward, his piercing gaze capturing Ronan's. "And once you've done all that, Carew, you march up to her, look her in the eyes, and tell her exactly how you feel. No hedging, no excuses. Lay your heart bare. If she accepts, she's yours. If not, then at least you will know you gave it your all."

Ronan let out a long breath, his resolve hardening. "You're all insufferable, you know that? But you are in the right of it. I cannot afford to hesitate any longer."

"Good," Westwood said, a faint smile tugging at the corners of his mouth. "Grace deserves a man who will fight for her."

"Does that mean I have your blessing?" If he were being honest, Westwood's blessing was what he feared would not be freely given.

"As long as you make Grace happy."

Ronan would die trying.

"And you," Rotham added with a rare grin, "deserve to be reminded that romance is not for the faint of heart. Now off you go, Carew. Win your lady."

As Ronan strode towards the door, Cunningham called after him, "And for goodness' sake, change and shave before you declare your undying love."

Ronan didn't reply, but as he closed the door behind him, he felt a faint smile tug at his lips. It seemed he had allies in this—and a second chance worth fighting for. He'd been afraid his friends would validate his fears of unworthiness. Now to go home, bathe, change, and plan.

As Ronan strode from the room, determination etched into every line of his face, the three men exchanged glances.

"Do you think he will succeed?" Rotham asked, his tone light but curious.

Westwood lifted his glass. "Faith told me Grace is already willing to have him, but I will enjoy seeing him grovel for once."

CHAPTER 21

The morning looked deceptively warm as sunlight streamed through the windows of Westwood House. Grace sat in the morning room with her embroidery, her stitches slow and uneven as her thoughts wandered. Theo and Evalina played with some knotted thread she'd tossed to them, while her sisters and Maeve dotted the room at their own tasks.

The monotony was broken by the sudden arrival of a footman, who carried an elegant bouquet of pink roses, freesia, ivy, and violets. Their fresh scent wafted gently through the air as he presented them to Grace.

"For you, miss," he announced, bowing slightly before withdrawing.

Grace's fingers stilled on the fabric, her brow furrowing as she set aside her work and reached for the flowers. Tucked among the blossoms was a small, folded note, its edges embossed with a simple yet elegant crest. Her heart quickened as she recognized the seal.

With trembling hands, she opened the note and read the neatly penned lines:

. . .

Dear Miss Whitford,

Would you please do me the honour of accompanying me on a drive this morning if you are not otherwise engaged? I will call for you at noon, should that be convenient to you.

Your obedient servant,
Carew

For a moment, she simply stared at the words. The note was simple, but it carried a weight that set her pulse racing. He was holding out an olive branch by asking to see her—so perhaps she had not ruined everything last night.

"Look! These flowers mean love, hope, sincerity, and fidelity, and there are love knots woven inside." Hope would know such things as she was the romantic one. Still, did the bouquet really hold such meaning? Had Carew chosen them with that in mind? It could be a coincidence.

Joy leaned over, her eyes sparkling with curiosity. "What is it, Grace? You look flushed. Pray tell."

"'Tis nothing," Grace replied too quickly, clutching the note to her chest and feeling a bit timid with Lady Maeve present. However, her evasiveness only piqued their interest further, and soon Hope and Faith joined the fray, each pressing her for details.

When she finally relented, holding up the note with a resigned sigh, the room erupted into a flurry of exclamations and advice.

"You must go, of course," Patience declared, ever practical.

"And wear something becoming," Joy added with a grin. "This is no time for drab grey."

Faith, more measured in her response, laid a hand on Grace's arm. "This is the chance you hoped for."

"It is from my brother? I knew it," Lady Maeve said with a satisfied smile.

At noon precisely, the sound of hooves and wheels on gravel drew Grace and the others to the window. There he sat, in a gleaming curricle pulled by a pair of matched bays, their coats shining like polished bronze in the afternoon sun. Ronan's posture was relaxed, his hands steady on the reins, but even from a distance, he was the most striking man she'd ever seen.

Her nerves, which had already been frayed by the morning's anticipation, threatened to unravel entirely as she adjusted her bonnet one final time and descended the stairs. She had chosen a gown of her favourite emerald green with delicate embroidery at the hem—simple yet flattering, at Joy's insistence—and a matching cloak to guard against the lingering chill.

When she stepped outside, the crisp air brought a faint colour to her cheeks. Ronan turned at the sound of her approach, his gaze softening as he took her in. He descended swiftly, tossing the reins to the groom, then offering his hand to help her into the curricle.

"Miss Whitford," he said, his voice low and steady, though there was a flicker of something more in his eyes—nervousness, perhaps? "You look lovely."

"Thank you," she replied quietly, her gloved hand resting lightly in his as she climbed into the seat. She settled beside him, hating the stiff formality of this exchange and longing for the easy way they'd known before.

The silence that followed was not unpleasant, but it was charged, Grace acutely aware of him as the curricle began to move. The bays, well-trained and spirited, responded to Ronan's light touch, their strides even as they pulled the carriage down the lane.

Grace kept her gaze fixed on the scenery, the gentle sway of the curricle and the rhythmic clatter of hooves doing little to calm her nerves. She was painfully aware of his nearness, of the way his shoulder or thigh brushed hers when they turned a corner.

"I hope the flowers were to your liking," he said at last, breaking the silence.

"They were lovely," Grace replied, her voice steadier than she had expected. "Thank you."

He nodded, his attention briefly on the horses before returning to her. "I was concerned they might be too plain. You deserve more than a handful of blooms."

Grace glanced at him, her brow furrowing slightly. "Simplicity is often the most elegant, my lord."

"Ronan," he corrected softly, his gaze unwavering.

Her cheeks warmed, and she looked away, the weight of his gaze almost too much to bear.

He smiled faintly, the tightness in his shoulders easing ever so slightly. "Thank you for coming, Grace. There are things I need to say—things I did not say properly the first time."

Her heart quickened, but she kept her voice even. "I am listening, sir."

And as the curricle carried them farther from the house, past the city and into the countryside, Grace braced herself for the words that might mend or break her heart entirely.

The curricle moved steadily along the winding country lane, the matched bays pulling with an effortless grace that opposed the tension-laden air between its two occupants. The countryside stretched out before them, the fields fallow and the trees barren. She sat composed, though her fingers twisted slightly in the folds of her cloak. She waited for something to cut the tension between them.

"I asked for your forgiveness last night."

Grace's gaze shifted to him, and knew she must be forthright. "I have thought about that a great deal, and I do not think you need my forgiveness, my lord," she replied quietly. "I understand you thought you were acting in my best interests."

Ronan glanced at her, his jaw tightening. "But I should like it just the same. I let fear and pride dictate my actions, and in doing so, I caused you pain."

"You acted as you thought best. I cannot fault you for wishing for my happiness."

"But that is where I failed," he said, his voice thick with emotion. "I did not ask you for your opinion." He drew the reins lightly, slowing the curricle and pulled it to the side of the road. "I convinced myself that pushing you away was the proper thing to do, but in truth I was a coward, too afraid to admit how much you mean to me."

Grace's breath caught, and she turned to him, her composure wavering. "Ronan…"

He stopped the curricle entirely, the horses stamping lightly as they came to a halt. Carew set the reins aside and turned to face her fully, his blue eyes bright with intensity. "I cannot bear the thought of losing you, Grace. Not to another man, not to the distance I put between us. I have spent weeks regretting my actions; all the moments I let slip away and every word I left unsaid."

Grace stared at him, her heart pounding in her chest. The vulnerability in his expression and the raw sincerity in his voice were unlike anything she had ever seen from him.

"I love you," he said, the words spilling forth as though he could not help himself. "I have loved you from the moment you held my great sword up to defend yourself, even before I had the sense to realize it. And if you will allow me, I will spend the rest of my life proving it to you."

Tears welled in Grace's eyes, and she raised a trembling hand to her lips.

"Say that you will give me a chance," he implored, his voice breaking slightly. "Say that you will let me make amends for my foolishness, that you will let me spend my life making you happy. Say that I have not thrown away the best thing that ever happened to me."

Grace's heart ached with the weight of his words, her emotions a tangled web of joy, fear, and longing. She reached out, her hand brushing lightly against his. "I was devastated when you sent me away, but I could never stop hoping."

Ronan's shoulders sagged with relief, and he took her hand in his, holding it as though it were the most precious thing in the world. "I will treasure you every day, Grace. That is my solemn vow."

Her lips curved into a faint smile, the tears spilling over as she whispered, "Now is a good time to kiss me, Ronan."

His lips slid into a sly smile. "Why did I ever think you were the quiet, shy one?"

"Perhaps I am just like one of those rare flowers that only blooms in the right conditions."

"I do not mind if you only bloom for me, but I am afraid now that your petals have unfurled, there will be no hiding your glory."

She shook her head. Such nonsense. "Stop talking, Ronan."

Even though she expected it, her breath hitched as Ronan leaned closer, his deep blue eyes searching hers with a tenderness that made her heart ache. She barely had time to register the warmth of his hand cradling her cheek before his lips brushed hers, soft and reverent. Her eyes fluttered closed, the world around them dissolving into only the two of them and that moment. The kiss deepened, tender and unhurried, each moment imbued with unspoken promises. When they parted, his forehead rested gently against hers. It was not the kiss of a man claiming what was his, but of one giving her his heart.

∽

RONAN KEPT his eyes on the winding road as the curricle bumped gently over the fallen leaves that blanketed the path. The trees on either side stood bare, their spindly branches reaching towards the pale sky, and the late-autumn air carried a sharp chill. Beside him, Grace tucked her gloved hands into her lap, her expression serene yet thoughtful. They had been driving for over an hour, and only now did she glance at him, her curiosity breaking through her composed exterior.

"Where are we going?" she asked at last, her tone tinged with amusement and intrigue.

He smiled, the corner of his mouth lifting. Grace's patience was one of her many virtues, though it had its limits, it seemed. "'Tis not much to look at in winter," he admitted, "but this has always been one of my favourite places to escape London."

Her brow furrowed slightly, but she said nothing more, her gaze shifting to the path ahead as the curricle rounded a bend. Ronan slowed the horses, his anticipation building as they approached the estate. When they passed through the gates, the drive opened to reveal the house: an elegant, sprawling manor of honey-coloured stone with ivy climbing its walls. Its modest grandeur fit the landscape perfectly, set amidst rolling fields that sloped gently towards the horizon.

Grace's breath caught, her hand instinctively tightening on his arm. "Oh," she whispered, her voice soft with awe. "It's beautiful."

He guided the curricle to a halt and leaped down, offering her his hand. "I hoped you might think so," he said as she stepped lightly to the ground. "This is Farleigh Manor, my mother's childhood home."

He led her through the grounds, pointing out the stables, the gardens now laid bare by the season, and the small orchard nestled beyond the house. Finally, they reached the edge of a pond, its surface rippling faintly in the breeze. The willow tree that stood beside it had shed its leaves, its stark branches arching gracefully over the water.

"This is my favourite spot," Ronan said quietly. "I have spent many an hour here, thinking, skimming stones and sometimes swimming."

Grace stepped closer to the water's edge, her cloak brushing against his as she tilted her head to study the landscape. "I can see why," she murmured. "It is so peaceful."

Ronan gestured to a nearby bench, and they sat together, the stillness wrapping around them like a warm quilt. He stole a glance at her profile, trying to decipher her thoughts.

He changed tactics. "I wanted you to see it before you made any decisions about where we might live."

Grace turned to him sharply, her eyes widening. "Live?"

Ronan gave her a small, teasing smile. "We can stay in London for the Season, but I thought…perhaps you might like it here, away from the chaos."

Grace's lips parted, her gaze flickering between him and the house. "You mean to say this could be our home?"

"If you wish it," he replied simply. "This place has always been a refuge for me. I thought it might be one for you as well."

For a moment, she said nothing, her expression as unreadable as her thoughts had been. Then she turned back to the house, her gaze softening. "It is quite, quite perfect."

Encouraged, Ronan reached for her hand, his tone growing more serious. "Grace," he began, his voice faltering slightly. "Will you give me your answer?"

She turned to him, her brows knitting together. "My answer to what?"

Ronan gave a rueful laugh, running a hand through his hair. "The question I have yet to ask properly, it seems."

A teasing light entered her eyes. "You have not actually asked," she said, her tone gently chiding. "You declared your intentions and left me to interpret the rest."

"You are maddening," he said, shaking his head with a smile, "but you are also right. Very well—I shall be precise."

Taking her hand in his, he leaned closer, his blue eyes searching hers. "Grace Whitford, will you do me the honour of becoming my wife? Of letting me spend my life proving myself worthy of you?"

Her teasing air fell away, replaced by a quiet intensity. She studied him for a long moment, her gaze flickering over his face as though seeking assurance.

"Yes," she said at last, her voice trembling but firm. "I will. But I have begun to loathe the word worthy. Just love me, Ronan, and that will be enough."

Ronan raised her hand to his lips, pressing a reverent kiss to her knuckles, his heart full. "You have made me the happiest man alive," he said, his voice thick with emotion.

Grace's cheeks coloured, but she did not look away. "And you," she replied, her voice just as soft, "have made me believe in happiness again."

The air around them seemed to hum with quiet contentment, as though the world itself paused to bear witness to this moment of joy. Ronan's hand, still cradling Grace's, trembled slightly—a rare admission of the depth of his feelings. He could scarcely believe that she had said yes, that this remarkable woman, with her gentle strength and quiet wit, had agreed to bind her life to his. She was everything opposite to him—everything he needed but didn't deserve.

Her gaze met his then, and the playful banter fell away, leaving only the quiet intensity of the moment. The gentle rustle of fallen leaves and the faint ripple of the pond seemed to fade into silence as Ronan lifted his free hand to cup her cheek. His thumb brushed lightly against her skin, and her breath hitched, her pulse rushing beneath his hand.

"Grace," he murmured, his voice barely audible, "I'm going to kiss you now."

"Finally," she murmured. "Happy am I that I did not have to beg." She leaned towards him, her lashes fluttering closed. Ronan needed no further encouragement. His lips met hers in a kiss that was at once tender and fervent, showing a love so profound it left him breathless.

Grace's hands rested lightly against his chest, the warmth of her embrace wrapping around him like a shield against the chill of the autumn air. How poetic he'd become in love! Of its own volition the kiss deepened, until they both drew back, their breaths mingling in the stillness.

Ronan searched her face, his blue eyes alight with wonder. "I feared I might wake and find this all a dream," he admitted softly.

Grace laughed, the sound low and melodious. "I assure you, I am quite real, though perhaps I should pinch you, to remove any lingering doubt."

He grinned, his gaze warm. "After the wedding, if you please."

They both laughed, the sound echoing softly over the water. Grace leaned back slightly, her gaze drifting over the landscape around them. "It is strange," she said, her voice thoughtful, "to think of all that has brought us here. Had I not slept through the ship's departure, had I not stayed aboard…"

"Had Flynn not been the scoundrel he was," Ronan added, scowling at the memory for a moment. "There are many twists of fate to consider."

"And yet," Grace continued, her tone brightening, "those same twists led to this moment. It is difficult not to feel grateful, even for the tribulations."

Ronan studied her, his heart swelling with appreciation. How she could find gratitude in the face of all she had endured was beyond him. "You find the light, even in the darkest of times," he said quietly. "It is one of the many things I admire about you."

Grace smiled, her cheeks tinged with pink from the cold. "Perhaps it is easier to find the light when one has to search for it."

For a moment, he was silent, reflecting. "I had not realized how empty my life had become until you appeared in it," he admitted, hearing the vulnerability in his words.

"Unexpectedly."

He chuckled. "You can have no notion what an understatement that is, my love. And you tempted me with the Grace Whitford I had yet to see. Then you left me."

"Only because you told me to!"

"There is that. Though you made me see that there is more to living than duty and revenge."

Grace tilted her head, looking at him tenderly. "And you showed me that there is strength in being vulnerable, even when it requires risk. You have been my anchor, Ronan, though I suspect you might not realize it."

He reached out, taking her hand gently in his. "If I have been your anchor, then you have been my compass, guiding me back to what truly matters."

They sat in companionable silence, enjoying the quiet harmony they had found together.

"Twists of fate, indeed," Ronan said at last, his tone lightening as he glanced at her with a mischievous glint in his eyes.

Grace laughed, her fingers tightening around his. "I would do it all again."

EPILOGUE

The little chapel on the Donnellan estate, tucked away amidst rolling emerald hills and ancient yews, had never seen such an array of joyful commotion. The late morning sun poured through the stained-glass windows, casting rays of coloured light upon the worn stone floor. The air was alive with the mingling scents of fresh flowers and polished wood, the quiet murmur of assembled guests weaving a gentle hum of anticipation.

Grace stood just outside the doors, her heart fluttering like a bird caught between freedom and the comforting nest.

She wore a delicate creation of ivory silk with lace trimming in her customary simple elegance. It fell softly to the floor, and her bonnet, adorned with fresh blooms, framed her face. Patience and Hope fussed over the folds of her gown, while Faith adjusted the veil with meticulous precision.

"Stop fidgeting, Grace," Faith chided, though her voice carried a smile. "You are a vision."

"I am trying to breathe," Grace retorted, feeling a mixture of nerves and humour. "Perhaps I ought to loosen my corset."

"Nonsense," Patience interjected. "You look perfect. Ronan won't be able to take his eyes from you."

It was not Ronan's gaze that made her nervous, although she did wish to look perfect for him. It was that she had never liked being the centre of attention.

The great oak doors creaked open, their sound resonating through the chapel like the prelude to an opera. A collective murmur rippled through the gathered guests as they stood up, and Grace, poised on the arm of Lord Westwood, drew in a steadying breath. The air inside the chapel was cool, carrying with it the faint scent of polished wood and fresh greenery. Sunlight streamed through the tall arched windows, casting dappled patterns on the stone floor.

Lady Donnellan sat in the front pew, dabbing her eyes discreetly with a lace handkerchief. Lord Donnellan sat beside her, his frail frame cloaked in heavy wool. Maeve was next to them but had turned in her seat, a lightness in her countenance that Grace had long hoped to see. She offered an encouraging nod, her smile radiating genuine affection.

On the opposite side, the entire Whitford, Westwood, and Rotham families had gathered, their presence a source of immeasurable comfort. Even both dowagers and the two aunts were in attendance. It meant everything to her that they had made the journey, and she reminded herself that everyone here belonged to her family.

Grace took her first step forward, her gown brushing lightly against the floor. Her heart thudded in her chest, but her steps were sure. If nerves were to overtake her, she resolved they would not show. She allowed her gaze to sweep forward, and her eyes found Ronan's.

He waited at the altar, in all his handsome splendour, his eyes gleaming with appreciation. It gave her the courage to keep walking.

His enchanting eyes drew her forward, unguarded and filled with an emotion so raw it made her heart ache. For a moment, everything else fell away.

At last, she reached him. Lord Westwood paused, his grip firm on her hand as he turned to Ronan. "See that you take care of her, Carew," he said gruffly, though his voice betrayed a thread of emotion.

His stern look eased slightly, tempered by the glimmer of approval in his gaze.

"With my life," Ronan replied, his voice solemn and steady.

As Lord Westwood stepped aside, Grace felt Ronan's warm hand clasp hers as they faced the vicar. The ceremony began, its simplicity a reflection of their shared desire for a day of quiet joy rather than pomp. The vicar's voice rang clear through the chapel, his words weaving the bonds that would unite them. Grace barely heard the murmurs of approval from the guests or the faint sniffles from her sisters in the pews. All she could feel was the warmth of Ronan's hand and the steady thrum of her heart.

When it came time for their vows, Ronan's voice was steady yet tinged with emotion, his words so heartfelt that Grace's throat tightened. She followed with her own vows, her voice soft but unwavering, each word carrying the truth of her feelings.

The vicar's pronouncement felt both timeless and immediate. "I now pronounce you man and wife."

Ronan lifted her hand and kissed it reverently, a seal of the vows they had made, and a promise of what was yet to come.

The late-autumn air was crisp, the gardens surrounding the chapel bathed in the warm glow of the setting sun as they returned to the castle for the wedding breakfast.

The great hall was strewn with greenery and lit by thousands of candles and blazing fires at either end.

Joy ensured the celebration was anything but staid. Her exuberant laugh carried over the conversations as she danced. Mr. Cunningham entertained the guests with his amusing commentary on the events, drawing laughter and good-natured ribbing in equal measure.

Lady Maeve approached them, her eyes sparkling with a mixture of mischief and affection. Dressed in Sardinian blue that complemented her dark hair, she looked happier than Grace had ever seen her. "There is no way back now, Brother," she teased, her tone light. "Fortunate it is that you have wed the most patient and forgiving woman alive."

Ronan slipped his arm around Grace and pulled her close. "I am indeed the fortunate one."

"Your time will come soon," Grace said softly.

Maeve gave a delicate laugh, though her cheeks flushed. "Let us hope that any suitor of mine proves as stubbornly persistent as Ronan. You are fortunate to find such a man, Grace."

"Indeed, I know it. But Maeve, I will gladly teach you all I know."

Ronan shook his head. "A dangerous alliance, I see. If you two continue in this vein, I may find myself entirely outmatched."

The string quartet began a waltz, and Maeve gave Grace an encouraging nudge. "Go, Sister. Enjoy your first dance as man and wife."

Grace allowed herself to be guided by Ronan to the centre of the dance floor, the warmth of his hand at her waist steadying her. As they joined the swirling couples, she looked up at him, feeling unmasked joy.

"Now I may hold you as close as I wish." Ronan arched a brow, a teasing smile tugging at his lips.

"Now the rogue returns," Grace retorted, her tone arch. "You will put me to the blush, my lord."

"Making you blush is a skill I treasure," he said, lowering his voice covertly. "You wear it so well. In fact, I shall now consider it one of my husbandly duties."

"I still enjoy dancing with you, my lord, even though you insist on teasing me so," Grace admitted.

"A captain must know how to navigate more than just the sea," he said with a wink. "Though the men are less appreciative of my waltzing prowess."

Grace chuckled. "I imagine so. I do not wish to think of them this day."

"Had it not been for them, you would have had no need to wield that big sword."

She laughed softly, her cheeks darkening to a deeper red she was certain. Thankfully, he stopped teasing her, and they moved together effortlessly, their steps perfectly aligned as they glided across the floor. Around them, the room seemed to fade, leaving only the music and the comforting strength of Ronan's presence. Soon enough, everyone would leave and she would at last have him to herself.

The music drew to a close, and Grace reluctantly stepped back. It was almost time to bid farewell to their guests and take time for themselves.

As Grace stood by Ronan's side, her heart felt wonderfully light. Finding her own love like her sisters' was more than she had ever dared to hope for.

Ronan looked down at her, his blue eyes filled with a warmth that made her breath hitch. His voice was a low murmur, meant only for her. "It feels as though I have found the only thing I ever truly needed." He plucked two glasses of champagne from the tray held by a passing footman and handed one to her. "To us."

She looked up at him, her eyes shining. "We have overcome a dreadful mistake, curses, and feuds, and managed to find a happy ending."

Ronan's lips curved into a smile, his gaze filled with both affection and reverence. "Aye," he said softly, his voice carrying deep emotion. "Only by Grace."

PREVIEW OF JOY'S STORY

*J*oy felt like a fraud as she stood in the glittering ballroom at Grosvenor Square. It was a study in opulence—diamonds glinting under the light of countless chandeliers, silken gowns swishing in rainbows of colours, and the murmur of conversation punctuated by bursts of laughter. None of it held the slightest appeal for her.

Standing near the refreshment table, she tugged absently at the too-tight sleeve of her lilac gown, a rare concession to fashion which left her feeling utterly unlike herself. Her wild locks had been subdued into an elegant coiffure with a thousand pins that dug into her scalp. She felt sure it would not survive the night, and her feet, garbed in delicate slippers, already pinched from the quadrille she had just suffered through.

"Cheer up, Joy," Patience whispered from her side, her voice laced with both amusement and sympathy. "It is the day of your birth. Surely you can find a shred of enjoyment in all this?"

Joy shot her elder sister a glare that lacked any real venom. "I should much rather be mucking out the stables than mincing about pretending to care for this nonsense."

Patience sighed, though the corners of her mouth twitched. "You might try smiling, at least. It's not so very dreadful."

Joy did not reply. The ballroom was a blur of indistinct shapes and shifting colours, and her head pounded from the effort of trying to distinguish one person from another. The Season would be one endless parade of such events, and her nerves were already wearing thin.

Her thoughts were interrupted by the arrival of Mr. Cunningham, who approached with his usual air of easy confidence.

"Miss Whitford," he said, bowing with exaggerated formality, his grin wide. "Suffering already?"

"Help me to escape, Freddy," she begged. "I do not know how you can stand these confounded events."

"It is all in how you look at them, my dear."

"There is more than one way?" She wrinkled her face, which she knew her governess would have scolded her for.

"You enjoy dancing."

"Yes, but not the stuffy ones where I must hold myself just so, and paste a false smile on." She imitated said posture and flattened her face.

Freddy laughed, as she had known he would. "You could do that, of course, or you could just be yourself."

"People already think I am outrageous."

He did not deny it. "Do you really wish to ensnare someone with whom you will have to pretend to be someone you are not for the rest of your life?"

"No, of course not." A feeling of panic threatened to make her flee the ballroom.

"Joy," he said lightly, though his tone held a note of concern, "are you quite well?"

"I am perfectly well," Joy said quickly. "My next partner approaches."

Joy found herself dreading the dance she had promised Lord Abernathy, a rather foppish young man who fancied himself a wit. As they stepped onto the floor, the patterns blurred and swirled before her eyes, and she stumbled, catching herself just in time.

A murmur rippled through the crowd, and Joy's cheeks burned. Abernathy, oblivious, chuckled and guided her clumsily through the steps, but her humiliation was complete. Now she had almost knocked down two Abernathys: mother and son. She could not endure an entire Season of this.

Freddy was waiting for her when Abernathy led her from the floor.

She looked down, avoiding his gaze. "The ballroom is crowded, and I was distracted."

"Hmm," was all he said, but his gaze lingered on her longer than she liked.

By the end of the evening, he sought her out, cornering her in a quiet alcove near the terrace. "Joy," he said softly, his usual banter absent. "When will you tell me what is troubling you?"

She opened her mouth to protest but faltered, the weight of her secret pressing down on her. "I don't know what you mean."

"I am your best friend," he said gently, his voice laced with a rare seriousness. "What is it? Your sight?"

She gasped and turned away. "'Tis nothing. Just…an inconvenience."

"It's not nothing," Cunningham said firmly. "Why have you not told anyone?"

Joy glared at him, but the fight drained out of her as quickly as it had risen. "What do you suggest I do? Call off the entire Season? Let everyone know how useless I am?"

"You are the least useless person I know," he said, his tone softening. "But you cannot face this alone. Let me help."

"The doctor said there is nothing to be done. I might be permanently blind soon."

As she looked up at him, his sincerity reflected in his steady gaze, something in Joy's heart shifted. Perhaps confiding in someone wasn't such a terrible idea.

AFTERWORD

Author's note: British spellings and grammar have been used in an effort to reflect what would have been done in the time period in which the novels are set. Yes, Jane Austen used -ize spellings, even though -ise is accepted now. While I realize all words may not be exact, I hope you can appreciate the differences and effort made to be historically accurate while attempting to retain readability for the modern audience.

Thank you for reading *Only By Grace*. I hope you enjoyed it. If you did, please help other readers find this book:

1. This ebook is lendable, so send it to a friend who you think might like it so she or he can discover me, too.
    2. Help other people find this book by writing a review.
    3. Sign up for my new releases at www.Elizabethjohnsauthor.com, so you can find out about the next book as soon as it's available.
    4. Come like my Facebook page www.facebook.com/Elizabethjohnsauthor or follow on Instagram @Ejohnsauthor or feel free to write me at elizabethjohnsauthor@gmail.com

ALSO BY ELIZABETH JOHNS

Surrender the Past

Seasons of Change

Seeking Redemption

Shadows of Doubt

Second Dance

Through the Fire

Melting the Ice

With the Wind

Out of the Darkness

After the Rain

Ray of Light

Moon and Stars

First Impressions

The Governess

On My Honour

Not Forgotten

An Officer Not a Gentleman

The Ones Left Behind

What Might Have Been

Leap of Faith

Finding Hope

The Gift of Patience

ACKNOWLEDGMENTS

There are many, many people who have contributed to making my books possible.

My family, who deals with the idiosyncrasies of a writer's life that do not fit into a 9 to 5 work day.

Dad, who reads every single version before and after anyone else—that alone qualifies him for sainthood.

Anj, who takes my visions and interpret them, making them into works of art people open in the first place.

To those friends who care about my stories enough to help me shape them before everyone else sees them.

Scott and Heather who helps me say what I mean to!

And to the readers who make all of this possible.

I am forever grateful to you all.